# The memories were bittersweet

*If she had let Richard make love to her.* How many times had Barbara contemplated the might-have-beens? How many times had she wondered how different her life might have been if she'd had the courage to give herself to him?

*It might have lasted.* They might have married, had babies, fought over the family finances, spent winter nights cuddled together under the covers of a king-size bed.

There would have been no broken hearts, no anger, no regrets, no wondering what it would have been like. There would have been no Dennis Wilson, no years of trying to conform to his expectations, no frustrating visits to doctors as she tried to conceive, no arguments over her work, no divorce.

*If she had let Richard make love to her....*

Dear Readers,

Writing about high school romance in *What Might Have Been* gave me an excellent excuse to reflect on some of the young men who added the spice of romance to my own youth.

There was Dick, whom I met at the skating rink. Not long after we began dating, he moved to New Orleans, and we eagerly wrote each other angst-filled letters.

Tommy, slightly dangerous and dashing, became a Marine. We were pen pals while he was in Vietnam.

Terry—tall, handsome Terry—had a bloodhound puppy and dreamed of becoming president. We argued over whether the word *rabbit* is pronounced "rabbit" or "wabbit."

Jim was cool, always invited to the best parties. We went cruising the hamburger stands in his mother's convertible when he could get it.

I met David—hazel-eyed David with the beautiful dimples— on a blind date because I was one of few girls my friend knew who was short enough for a guy five foot six. I took my first airplane flight—all of forty-five minutes—to go with him to his fraternity formal, and he took me to my senior prom.

And the college men…! John, a talented artist, made me one-of-a-kind greeting cards. Jerry took me on my first motorcyle ride. James wangled press passes to the rerelease of *Gone With the Wind*.

And then I met Rusty—tall, blond, blue-eyed Rusty who drove a Mustang, taught me to shoot a rifle, introduced me to Mexican food and tried to teach me to surf. Rusty and I laughed a lot when we were together.

A quarter of a century later, Rusty and I are still together and still laughing a lot. But I don't consider all those pre-Rusty loves to be lost. They're still with me, in that part of the heart reserved for tender memories. I'd like to think maybe a little of me lingers in their hearts, too.

Yours sincerely,

Glenda Sanders

# WHAT MIGHT HAVE BEEN
## GLENDA SANDERS

*Harlequin Books*

TORONTO • NEW YORK • LONDON
AMSTERDAM • PARIS • SYDNEY • HAMBURG
STOCKHOLM • ATHENS • TOKYO • MILAN
MADRID • WARSAW • BUDAPEST • AUCKLAND

The author wishes to express her appreciation to
Amy and Joseph, who shared information about Florida
adoption law and prenatal sonograms, respectively.
A special thank-you goes to Cynthia Holt, who answered a
multitude of questions, from the mundane to the sublime,
about the work and ethics of guidance counselors.

ISBN 0-373-25593-4

WHAT MIGHT HAVE BEEN

# Prologue

THE KISS WAS one of invitation, frank and unmistak-able. She pressed her body against his in the most pro-vocative way possible and darted her tongue back and forth against the roof of his mouth with suggestive rhythm. Finally she tore her mouth from his and tilted her head back slightly—far enough to ask the crucial question with her eyes.

Richard had not planned on this. He wasn't entirely sure he wanted it. He searched his memory for her name, a name still new and unfamiliar on his tongue, and said it tentatively.

She pressed her pelvis harder into his. "You're not going to try to tell me you're not interested."

A denial would only contradict what his sex-starved body was telling her. It had been more than a year since he'd been with a woman. Still, he was a bit befuddled by the swiftness of it all, and he said nothing.

It was supposed to have been a routine closing.

"If you're worried about responsibility, I'm on the pill. And I brought the proper safety equipment."

His incredulity must have shown because she said, "Does that surprise you? You're a nice-looking man. I'm attracted to you and you're not—" she wiggled against him and smiled smugly "—indifferent to me."

Still, he didn't speak.

"We're mature, unattached adults. If we're responsible, where's the harm? Why not enjoy each other's company?"

She was not beautiful, but she was attractive. And the roof of his mouth still tingled from her artful kiss.

*More than a year—*

He answered with action instead of words, dipping his head to hers and plundering her mouth as she'd plundered his. She was already tearing at his clothes, pulling his shirt from his trousers. He did the same with her blouse and soon they were touching, palms to bare backs.

Minutes later they were on the couch, Richard's doubts and inhibitions cast aside with their clothing. He was only human, after all.

He was too preoccupied to hear the door opening or the footsteps in the entryway. It took the gasp of shock and the mortified "Daddy!" to make him aware enough to look up—just in time to catch a fleeting glimpse of a retreating female figure.

# 1

THE STUDENT SEATED across from guidance counselor Barbara Wilson wore jeans, an oversize sweatshirt and sneakers. Her hair was long and wavy, her bangs moussed to resemble a cockscomb. She sat with her head slightly bowed and her shoulders slumped, clutching the handle of her large denim bag the way a small child might a security blanket. Though she was polite and responsive to Barbara's questions, she never lifted her eyes.

Her name was Missy Benson. She was sixteen years old, a member of the junior class and an honor student. And she was pregnant.

"You've applied for the home study program for the rest of the semester," Barbara said.

"Mmm-hmm." Missy accompanied the response with an all-purpose teenage shrug.

The girl was exceedingly uncomfortable, Barbara was sure. She did not know Missy well, but the times she had spoken to her previously, the girl had been much more outgoing.

"Did your doctor tell you that you'd have to restrict your activities during your pregnancy?" Barbara asked.

Missy shook her head.

"You're not due until mid-June," Barbara continued. "Unless you have some unusual medical problem, you shouldn't have any trouble attending school for the entire semester. We could schedule a study hall either before or after your lunch and you could rest in the nurse's office if you needed to."

Silence. Teenage silence. The bane of guidance counselors and parents throughout human history. Barbara waited until it was obvious Missy was not going to respond before asking, "Don't you think you'd get lonely at home all that time?"

Missy shrugged her shoulders as if to say she didn't care. Barbara suspected that she cared very much. "Are you afraid of being embarrassed?" she asked gently.

"Sort of."

Barbara let her stew for a moment, then said, "Most of your friends already know about your pregnancy, don't they?"

Barbara knew they did; she'd heard about Missy's pregnancy through the student grapevine a week before the application for home study came across her desk.

"I guess so," Missy mumbled.

A mumble was better than a grunt. Encouraged, Barbara said, "It was probably bad at first, but once everyone got over the shock, it's probably not so bad anymore."

Missy remained silent, but she was listening.

"Wouldn't you rather be here at school with your friends than hiding out at home?"

Another shrug.

Barbara waited a moment, then asked, "It wasn't your idea to stay at home, was it?"

Missy's words burst forth in a rush. "My dad says the kids will all make fun of me. He says I'd be uncomfortable."

"What do you think?"

"I guess he's right. I mean, I'm going to be fat, and I might walk funny."

Barbara smiled. Reassuringly, she hoped. "Maybe a little funny, toward the end. But if your friends teased you—I'm talking about your real friends, Missy—if they teased you, it would be the friendly type of teasing, sort of like they'd tease you if you got a bad haircut or spilled spaghetti in your lap."

Missy shifted uncomfortably, a sure sign to Barbara that she was listening. And thinking. Tentatively, Barbara said, "Teenagers need to be around other teenagers, Missy. Your friends can help you feel like you're still a part of things."

She gave Missy an opportunity to speak, but the girl only stared at her hands as she worried the handle of the denim bag.

"The longer you're out of school, the harder it's going to be to get back into the routine when you come back," Barbara said. "Don't you want to try staying in school?"

Missy chewed on her lower lip.

"If you stay, you can always change your mind later on, if you get too tired or feel too uncomfortable."

"But my dad—"

"Did you tell your father how you felt?"

Missy shrugged miserably.

Barbara sighed. "That's what I thought. Missy, I'm sure your father only wants to protect you, but sometimes it's not easy for parents to know the best way to protect their children. Especially in a difficult situation. Maybe if he knew how you felt and what the experts say—"

For the first time Missy's gaze met Barbara's. "Would you tell him, Ms. Wilson? He'd listen to you."

Barbara smiled. "I'd be happy to talk to your father, Missy."

The girl's "Thank you" was heartrending.

Barbara stood and walked to the side of her desk. "We've done about all we can do until I've had a chance to talk to him. I'll make the appointment as soon as possible."

Missy rose, ready to bolt.

*So young,* Barbara thought. *And so vulnerable.* And at that moment, so totally alone.

"You know, Missy, sometimes what we need more than anything else in the whole world is a big hug. Have you ever felt that way?"

"Oh, Ms. Wilson," Missy said, releasing a sob as she rushed into Barbara's arms. "My dad thinks I'm awful."

Barbara hugged her, rocked her as she would a small child, stroked her back. "I'm sure he's upset, Missy, but that doesn't mean he thinks you're awful. He's probably just scared."

"Scared?" Raising her head, Missy wiped her eyes with the back of her hand.

"Didn't you know that parents get scared?" Barbara asked as she offered Missy a tissue from the box on her desk. "Parents want to protect their children. They don't want anything bad to happen to them. And when something does, they feel bad, because they couldn't stop it. And that scares them. Your whole world has been turned upside down and inside out. And so has his."

Missy took a tissue and blotted her nose. "He's ashamed of me."

"Did he say that?"

"He didn't have to," Missy sniffed. "He doesn't want anyone to see me."

Barbara gave Missy another quick hug. "I'm sure your father wants to do what's best for you. He doesn't realize how understanding your friends would be. I'll explain it to him."

Missy sniffed. "Thanks."

"I hope..." Barbara said, then paused to organize her thoughts. "It's not always easy for parents and kids to talk when they're in an emotional situation. Sometimes you start arguing, instead of talking, or it's easier just not to say anything, but I hope you'll try to talk to your father and tell him anything you might be feeling."

Missy squared her shoulders and drew in a ragged breath, then nodded.

Barbara felt the girl's pain, her confusion, her desperation. And she knew that Missy didn't believe that talking to her father would do any good at all. She put her hands on Missy's shoulders. "Missy, I want you to know that any time you need to talk to someone, or just feel like a hug, you can come see me. Okay?"

"Okay."

"Sometimes I might be in a conference. You might have to wait a few minutes, but you just tell Mrs. Dinker you're on my 'anytime' list, and I'll see you as soon as I can."

"Thanks, Ms. Wilson."

"That's what I'm here for," Barbara said under her breath as Missy made a rabbit-into-the-hole teenage exit.

Sagging against the back of her chair, Barbara released a ragged sigh. Counseling pregnant students left her drained. They were so young, so confused. Children having children.

Children having *unwanted* children. The irony always cut deeply. To these pregnant children, pregnancy was a crisis; to Barbara, a childless, single woman pushing her thirty-fifth birthday, pregnancy was a precious gift that had been denied her.

There had been a time when she'd tried to become pregnant. She'd wanted a child very badly. Dennis had wanted a child, too. After all, it was the accepted thing to do, the societal norm, and Dennis always did the accepted thing.

But there had been no pregnancy and no child, and most of Barbara's hope of having one had died with the demise of her marriage. What was left of that hope had been eroding steadily in the five years since.

Barbara's life was full. There was no shortage, she had discovered, of young people who needed a kind word, a nonjudgmental sounding board, or an occasional hug. She had an entire school filled with students, most of whom, sooner or later, would need her in one way or another. But the ache, the yearning to have a child of her own, remained coiled inside her,

ready to emerge and sadden her when she saw a baby—
or a teenager carrying an unwanted child.

Barbara forced her attention to Missy Benson's personal file. Missy Benson. Grade eleven. Honor student. Student council representative for three years. School choir. Mother: Deceased. Father: Richard Benson, Realtor.

*Richard Benson.* The blood drained from Barbara's face, and she scolded herself for reacting like one of her angst-driven teenage students. There must be hundreds of Richard Bensons in the country. She'd probably find half a dozen or so in the local phone directory. The odds against Missy's father being the Richard Benson she'd known years ago, hundreds of miles away in a small town in Georgia, were substantial. And yet—his daughter would be a teenager now. Some quick calculations told her the child would be . . . almost seventeen. Missy's age. What if he turned out to be the same man?

Trembling, she lowered her face into her hands and exhaled wearily, then drew in a calming breath and told herself to look at the situation objectively. The world wouldn't stop rotating if she came face-to-face with an old boyfriend, not even one—

*One she'd loved with all her heart. One she'd once felt closer to than any other person on earth. One who'd made the earth tremble with his kisses. The one who'd broken her heart.*

Richard Benson had been more than a boyfriend. But he hadn't been her lover. After all the years, that fact still hurt, and it still haunted.

*If she had let Richard make love to her.* How many times had she contemplated the might-have-beens? How many times had she wondered how different her life might have been if she'd had the courage to give herself to him?

*It might have lasted.* They might have married, had children, traded shifts comforting teething children in the middle of the night, fought over the family finances, spent winter nights cuddled together under the covers of a king-size bed.

There would have been no broken hearts, no anger, no regrets, no wondering what it would have been like. There would have been no Dennis Wilson, no years of trying to conform and do what was expected, no frustrating visits to doctors as she tried to conceive children, no arguments over her work, no divorce.

*If she had let Richard make love to her.* She sloughed off the speculation and sat up straighter in her chair, running her finger over the personal information form until she found Richard Benson's office number.

Her voice sounded almost normal as she told the receptionist at Benson Realty her name and asked to speak to Missy's father.

IN THE CORNER office at Benson Realty, Richard had to stop reading the contract he was reviewing to answer the buzzing intercom. "Yeah, Margaret. What is it?"

"I know you wanted me to screen your calls, but there's a Mrs. Wilson on line two who says she's calling from Missy's school," his receptionist said.

Richard's stomach knotted. *Missy's school?* Oh, God, what if it were a medical emergency? "I'll take it," he said. He barely finished the words before punching the button that would connect him to the caller. "Richard Benson," he barked into the receiver.

"Mr. Benson, this is—" Barbara had to swallow before she could go on. She honestly couldn't tell whether the voice was the one she'd been dreading. Anticipating. *Hoping for, damn it!* "Barbara Wilson, the eleventh-grade counselor at Missy's school."

"Is Missy all right?"

"She's fine," Barbara said. *Aside from being pregnant and terrified and feeling like a pariah, she's perfectly fine.* "She just left my office. There's no emergency."

She sensed his relief.

"I've been reviewing Missy's application for home study, and I'd like to discuss it with you. Could you possibly come to the school for about half an hour tomorrow?"

*Would you let me see your face to see if it's the one I've been remembering for seventeen years?*

Richard relaxed. A little. He hadn't relaxed completely since Missy had come to him with the news that she suspected she was pregnant. He sometimes wondered if he'd ever fully relax again. "Morning would be best for me," he said.

"Eight-thirty?"

"Perfect."

Barbara froze. Froze, and slid back in time. Froze, and was sitting again in Richard's aging Mustang. Now it would be a classic. Then it was just old. Richard had unbuttoned her blouse, mastered the front closure on her bra.

He was the first boy she'd allowed to see her breasts.

His breath had caught in his throat. "Perfect," he'd whispered.

Eight-thirty tomorrow morning was *perfect*.

"I'll see you tomorrow morning, then," she said hoarsely. Her hand was trembling when she hung up the phone.

"Well, now you know," she said aloud, with a sigh. Somehow she got through the rest of the day with a semblance of normalcy.

As planned, she stopped at the drugstore on her way home from work to buy toothpaste, which was on sale. As always when she went to the drugstore, she looked around for bargain items or grooming products the supermarket didn't stock. But when she placed her purchases on the counter to be checked, she was shocked by what she'd put into the cart on this particular visit: a pouch of the expensive hair conditioner that made her hair shiny when she took the time to use it, scented bath oil, mascara and lipstick.

The mascara was especially surprising. She'd been out of the cosmetic for weeks and hadn't bothered to shop for it. She wore very little makeup to school. But tomorrow she was going to be seeing Richard Benson, and so today she was buying mascara—and lipstick that matched the cranberry scarf she always wore with her gray suit. She couldn't possibly wear anything tomorrow except her gray suit. It was understated enough not to look conspicuous when she wore it to school; yet it was the most flattering thing in her closet.

Not that it mattered.

Barbara watched the clerk slide the purchases over the electronic scanner one by one and frowned. Who was she trying to kid, anyway? It mattered. It mattered a lot. Maybe because everything between Richard and her had ended so badly. Or, maybe, because it had ended in so much pain, and it had ended without resolution.

*"I want you so much, Barbara."* This, breathlessly, as Barbara pushed his hand away from the zipper of her jeans.

*"I know, Richard."* Just as breathless and desperate. *"And I want to say yes. It's just . . . I'm scared. I'm not ready yet."*

And then, with an ugly inflection of frustration, *"Well, maybe I should find someone who is ready. Someone who's grown up enough to please a man."*

The words had cut like a knife. Barbara had choked back tears and thrust her head high. "If that's what you want, then go ahead. Find someone else."

"Maybe I will."

"Maybe you ought to."

"Don't you think I can?"

"Sure. If that's what you want."

*A man.* He'd been all of nineteen years old. With the perspective of hindsight and maturity, Barbara could almost see the ironic humor in his words. She might even have found the memory amusing—if it hadn't held the power, still, to wound her so deeply.

Because Richard *had* found someone else. He'd found Christine, whom everyone knew was a very obliging girl to frustrated *men.* And he'd paraded her into the stadium for the homecoming football game.

The news had spread like wildfire. Richard had dumped Barbara for a tramp. Barbara, who'd gone to the game without a date, confident that Richard would show up and they would make up, and everything would be rosy again.

The next thing she'd heard about Richard was that he'd married Christine on his Christmas break to give their child a name. She'd heard later on that they'd had a baby girl, and that Richard had dropped out of the state university to work full time.

The next year Barbara had gone away to college, where she'd met Dennis. Dennis hadn't been passionate like Richard. He couldn't make Barbara feel the things Richard had made her feel. That had been the reason she'd felt safe dating him; eventually, it was the main reason she divorced him.

And now Richard was living in Orlando, too. Funny how things worked out.

UNSURE how she was going to react to the sight of him, Barbara arrived at her office early the next morning. She wanted to be in familiar surroundings and prepared when she saw him, not caught off guard on the sidewalk or in the hallway.

Shiny-haired, softened, moisturized, perfumed and mascaraed, too nervous to chance a cup of coffee and too wound up to keep from fidgeting, she sat behind her desk and pondered all the possibilities of the imminent meeting.

Seventeen years. He could be fat and bald.

*Yeah. Sure.*

What would he say? What should she say?

What if he didn't recognize her? How would she handle that? Laugh gently and say, "Oh, by the way, my name used to be Simmons"? Not mention it and hope he didn't notice?

*Oh, God, what if she told him who she was and he didn't even remember her?* What if the two years they'd spent as sweethearts had meant nothing to him? What if he'd never even given her a thought in all the years since that horrible football game?

*What if he recognized her, and everything was exactly as it had been seventeen years ago?*

Barbara wasn't sure which prospect terrified her the most.

When he arrived, five minutes early, she was glad she'd had the benefit of forewarning. He was not fat. He was not bald. He was simply Richard, older and unforgivably improved by age.

Laugh lines had given his face character, and his hair, no longer bleached by the sun, was darker. The twenty pounds he'd picked up had been much kinder to him than the ten pounds Barbara had acquired; they gave him a look of solidity and authority he hadn't possessed as a skinny adolescent.

She would have known him anywhere.

And she knew the instant he recognized her. It was in the middle of saying her name, after he'd stepped tentatively into her office. "Ms. Wil—"

He froze, fought for equilibrium—then finished, "My, God. Barbara?"

"Hello, Richard."

She had forgotten how he could look at a woman, as though he were taking in every detail of her. Or perhaps, as a seventeen-year-old, she'd been too innocent to fully appreciate the sensual quality of what he was doing. She'd just thought he had a neat way of looking at her and making her feel all warm inside.

Now, as a woman, she appreciated his gaze for what it was, and her insides still melted under the sizzle of it.

For a long moment—an eternity—they stared at each other. Remembering. Reacting. The small room filled with tension, until the very air seemed heavy as Barbara tried to breathe.

And then, at last, Richard broke the stalemate.

"You could have warned me," he said.

# 2

BARBARA.

In all the dark, quiet moments haunted by the memories of her, Richard had never envisioned her any other way than the way she'd been the last time he'd seen her. Why hadn't he realized she would grow older, too?

Her face was more mature, but still beautiful. Her hair was conservatively styled, but still shiny. It would be soft, too; he remembered the way it had felt when he'd touched it.

She was slightly heavier, but the weight filled out curves that had been mere promises in her youth. And her eyes—

They were exactly the same: large, green, expressive. He saw apprehension in their depths as she forced a smile.

"I wasn't sure," she said.

"That I would remember you?" he asked, bemused by that prospect.

"That you were the same Richard Benson."

"Your name is different."

Just for an instant, sadness veiled her eyes. "I was married."

"Was?"

"It didn't last."

"I'm sorry." He truly was. Lord, how could a man smart enough to marry Barbara be stupid enough to divorce her?

"It's been over for years," she said.

Silence crept between them until, finally, she indicated the chair facing her desk. "We need to talk about Missy."

Richard nodded. "Of course."

*Of course.* Oh, God, she knew about Missy. It was her job to know.

Richard's jaw clenched. His lips compressed into a grim line. Why did it have to be Barbara of all people? What kind of father did she think he was? What kind of human being had she thought he was seventeen years ago when he'd jilted her for the town tramp because she wouldn't sleep with him?

He felt naked suddenly, stripped of pretenses and dignity, like a knight caught by an enemy without mail or armor. And then he looked at Barbara, dwarfed by the sturdy wooden teacher's desk, and wondered how he could equate her, even symbolically, with an enemy. He searched her eyes for censure but found only concern.

She opened a file folder, glanced at it briefly, then looked at Richard's face and smiled. "Missy's a wonderful girl, Richard."

Richard acknowledged the comment with an awkward shrug, wondering where the conversation was going. It would have been easier to talk to a stranger than to Barbara. She knew too much about him.

"I have her application for home study here," Barbara said, crisply professional.

Richard nodded.

Barbara's gaze met his levelly. "Can you tell me why you think home study is necessary?"

"Missy's an excellent student," Richard said. "I don't want this...situation to jeopardize her graduating with her class."

Barbara nodded.

It was a professional nod, Richard thought, like a doctor listening to a list of symptoms. "She wants to go to college," he said a bit defensively.

"With her grades, she should do very well in college."

Sensing her hesitation, Richard asked, "Is there a problem with the home study?"

"Not a problem, exactly. A concern. I'm not sure home study is the best option for Missy."

Richard plunged his hand through his hair, then absently massaged his neck. "I don't want her to lose a semester."

"There's no reason she would," Barbara said. "Unless the baby's early, there's no reason she couldn't finish out the school year in the classroom."

"But she's going to be—" He exhaled, frustrated. "You know what I mean. I don't want her to be embarrassed."

"Do you want her to be ashamed?"

"What's your point?"

"Have you considered what kind of message you're giving Missy by forcing her into hiding?"

"God," Richard said in a prolonged rush of breath. "I don't know what to do anymore. I want to protect her, but—"

"It's impossible to protect children when they start turning into adults. Maybe you could focus on supporting her instead."

"I seem to be muddling that, too," he said miserably.

Barbara smiled encouragingly. "You're probably doing a much better job than you think you are. You wouldn't be here if you weren't concerned. And Missy wouldn't be the person she is if you weren't doing something right."

*And she wouldn't be in the condition she's in if I'd been a better father,* Richard thought bitterly. "You think Missy should stay in school instead of having instruction at home?"

"Yes, I do. Missy will be undergoing a lot of change as her pregnancy progresses, emotionally as well as physically. There'll be hormonal fluctuations, as well. Her self-esteem will be extremely fragile. If you force her into hiding, she's going to feel that you're ashamed of her."

"But the kids—"

"Studies have shown that teenagers can provide a valuable support network to their pregnant peers. And the closer Missy stays to her normal routines when she's pregnant, the easier it'll be for her to return to those routines following the birth of the baby. I know it's going to sound ludicrous, but however unfortunate Missy's situation is, the timing of her due date couldn't be more opportune in terms of not disrupting the school year."

"You're right," he said bitterly. "It sounds ludicrous."

"I talked to Missy, and I think she'd prefer to stay in the classroom."

"How could Missy possibly imagine what it's going to be like when she's blown up like a blimp?"

Barbara chuckled at his naïveté. "I don't think you're giving her enough credit. Kids today know a lot more than we did at their age." She leaned forward. "Look, Richard, if you let her stay in the classroom, she can change her mind at any point along the way. But until it's her idea to leave, my advice would be to allow her to stay in school, where she'll have daily contact with her friends."

Frowning, Richard pondered the advice. Of course he would do whatever she recommended. She was the expert in the field, and he—

He released a sigh. God knew, he was no expert. If he were an expert, he wouldn't be sitting here discussing options for Missy's schooling while she was pregnant.

Barbara was sitting behind her desk, giving him an understanding look. Despite the age, the different hairstyle, she was the same as always. Gentle. Caring. It was not surprising that she had chosen a job that surrounded her with people. He was curious, suddenly, about her life since he'd seen her, all those intervening years. She'd spoken authoritatively about parenting and protecting and supporting, but she couldn't have a child anywhere near Missy's age.

"Do you have children?" he asked.

"No. We tried, but—" If he hadn't known her so well, if he hadn't been looking at her face with such rapt attention, he might have missed the sadness that veiled her eyes as she gently shrugged her shoulders.

"That's too bad," he said.

She smiled. "I've got all the kids I need right here in this building."

Richard nodded. She probably took in troubled students the way some people took in stray puppies.

She referred to the file folder again, skimming the information before returning her attention to Richard. "According to Missy's personal information card, her mother is deceased."

Richard's gaze fell to his hands. "She was killed in an automobile accident when Missy was seven."

"I'm sorry."

"Missy hadn't seen her mother in over a year, but she took it quite hard." He paused, swallowed. "I think she'd always believed that Christine would do some kind of magical turnaround and behave like a real mother. When Christine was killed, she had to give up all hope of that happening."

"You and Christine—"

"Christine didn't care much for motherhood. She cared even less about being a wife."

"I'm sorry things didn't work out for you."

Richard chortled bitterly. "That's generous of you, considering."

Barbara squared her shoulders. "That was a long time ago, Richard. We were just kids."

An uncomfortable silence descended between them. Finally, Barbara said softly, "I never wished you any unhappiness, Richard."

"No," he said. "You wouldn't do that. But then, you didn't have to. I rushed off in pursuit of unhappiness without needing anybody's wishes."

Her smile was gentle. "But you have Missy."

"Yes." *And he'd done his best. But his best hadn't been good enough to keep him from bungling parenthood the same way he'd bungled marriage.*

"Does Missy have a woman she's close to? Someone she confides in?"

Richard shook his head. "No. Not since—" He drew in a steeling breath. "My mother lived with us until last year. She more or less raised Missy after Christine took off. But even if she were still here, I'm not sure Missy would feel comfortable confiding in her. My mother—"

Barbara grinned. "From what I can remember about your mother, she wasn't exactly liberal-minded."

"Then you see the problem."

"It's not unusual for teens to pull away from their parents. When there's a gap of two generations instead of one, sometimes the rift is more pronounced."

She paused briefly. She was in her counselor mode again, Richard noticed.

"Missy needs someone she feels comfortable talking to now. Since there's no other woman in your home, I think you should consider some professional counseling."

"I'll talk to her about it," Richard said.

"Good," Barbara said and, sighing, let her shoulders relax against the back of her chair. "You know, I'm always hesitant to suggest counseling. Some people are resistant to the idea. I'm glad you're not."

"I want what's best for Missy."

"That's obvious." So much was obvious to her as she looked at him: his desperation and parental guilt over Missy's condition, his love and concern for his daughter, and his frustration over not being able to take away all her problems. She saw parents every day with smaller problems and larger problems. But none of them were Richard Benson. And very few of them seemed as isolated with their problems as Richard seemed to her.

She fought for a professional objectivity and detachment she did not feel. "I have a list of counselors if Missy wants to see one. Or you could ask your family doctor or minister for a referral."

"I'd trust your recommendations. You specialize in teenagers."

Barbara nodded, opened a drawer and flipped through hanging files until she found the right folder and slid a sheet of paper across her desk. "Let me know what you decide in any event. And if there's any way I can help you, please don't hesitate—"

She stopped and gave Richard a strange look. He was grinning. "Did I miss something?"

"I just can't get over the fact that it's you behind that desk."

She smiled. "One of those strange coincidences. I think it falls under the heading of 'small world.'"

His intense gaze settled on her face. "You should be out in the hall taking your books out of locker two-two-four instead of sitting behind a counselor's desk."

"Locker number two-two-four. How did you ever remember that?"

"I had two-two-six, remember?"

"Until you graduated and left me at the mercy of that nerd who got it after you."

They passed a moment in silence, remembering. Finally, Richard shook his head. "Did either of us really think we'd ever grow up and become adults?"

"We didn't have a lot of choice," Barbara reflected sadly. "Peter Pan is a myth."

"Barbara." Her name. His voice. The sound of it tickled over her senses and stirred memories. Dangerous memories. Memories that didn't belong in her office when she was counseling the parent of a student.

Taking the coward's way out, she glanced at her watch. "I have another parent coming in," she said. "If there's nothing else—"

He picked up on the cue and rose. Automatically he extended his hand. "Thank you for your interest in Missy."

But as she placed her hand in his, his fingers tightened around hers and his eyes settled on her face. "God, Barbara. Who'd have thought we'd run into each other like this, three hundred miles from home in the Orlando suburbs?"

"My friends call me Barb now," she said.

"My friends call me Rick."

She laughed gently. "I guess we really did grow up."

Reluctantly he released her hand. "You've got another parent waiting."

"Let me know what you decide about the counseling."

Richard nodded, then left, walking as though his feet were heavy weights.

Barbara waited until he was out of sight, then sank into her chair, hugging herself as a tremor of reaction shivered through her. She had always wondered how she'd feel if she saw Richard again.

Well, she'd seen him, and now she knew.

She felt sixteen. And very much in love.

*It'll pass,* she assured herself. It was just a combination of memory and nostalgia. All she had to do was laugh at herself and how silly she was being and she'd get over it.

In another seventeen years or so.

In the meantime she had plenty to keep her busy, including the concerned parent waiting in the reception area.

Richard lingered hauntingly in her mind for the rest of the day, the evening, throughout the night. Over and over, she relived the magic and splendor of their relationship, the hurt and bitterness of his betrayal. She was no more successful at escaping the image of Richard as he'd been in her office: concerned, frustrated, alone, and plagued by guilt and confusion. She thought of Missy, too—pregnant, vulnerable, motherless Missy. Richard's child.

And she tried very hard not to wonder whether, if she'd had a child with Richard, her child would have looked like Missy.

ONCE OR TWICE the next morning, it crossed Barbara's mind that Richard might call to let her know what Missy had decided about going into counseling, but she wasn't expecting to find his name on the sign-in list of people wanting to see her later that morning. Her surprise must have been evident as she scanned the waiting room for him, because he quickly rose and walked over to her. "I took a chance that you'd have time to talk. Just for a minute."

Her gaze locked with his. She never refused to talk to a parent, but as they stood looking at each other, they both knew that his presence there extended beyond the concern of a parent for a student. "If you don't mind waiting—"

"I'll wait."

Later, in her office, she said, "I hope you don't mind if I nibble while we talk." A paper bag from her drawer yielded a sandwich, a bag of chips and an apple.

"I didn't mean to take up your lunch hour."

"It's not the first time I've eaten at my desk. It probably won't be the last. Oh, and you can take off your coat, if you'd like. It's not a formal meal."

Though he'd seldom worn suits when she'd known him, the way he moved as he removed his blazer and draped it over the back of his chair was hauntingly familiar. She had known him so very well.

She tossed the apple to him, baseball style.

Catching it easily, he eyed it critically, then grinned. "Trying to tempt me, Mrs. Wilson?"

"Just being polite," she assured him. "I'd offer you my sandwich, but you can go to a drive-through on the way back to your office, and I'm stuck on campus."

"If I had realized, I'd have brought baby quiches and strawberries in a wicker basket."

Her laughter was comfortable, genuine. "How often do you have quiche for lunch?"

He pretended to consider the question seriously. "At least once or twice a . . . lifetime."

He hadn't lost his sense of humor. *He was still Richard.* The realization brought the sting of tears to Barbara's eyes.

The Richard who'd ripped her heart to shreds, she reminded herself as she took a bite of her sandwich.

"I talked to Missy about counseling," Richard said tentatively.

"What'd she say?"

"She was agreeable—with a stipulation."

Curious, Barbara abandoned her sandwich. "What's the stipulation?"

"She wants you to counsel her."

"Me? But—"

Richard shrugged. "That's why I wanted to talk to you. I don't know the protocol, but Missy—" He sighed. "Missy thinks she could talk to you, and she was adamant about not wanting to go to a stranger. So I told her I'd ask you about it."

"But I'm not licensed for that kind of counseling," she said.

"I would pay you, of course."

"It's not a question of money. I couldn't possibly take money for counseling a student."

"It's not as though she's in danger of becoming an ax murderer," Richard said.

"I couldn't give her the type of attention she needs here at school."

"She feels comfortable with you," Richard argued persuasively.

"I suppose we could work something out once or twice a week."

"Thank you," Richard said, obviously relieved. "Barbara—"

She looked at him expectantly, but he just shook his head. "Just . . . thank you." He sighed dismally. "Sometimes I'm more confused than Missy."

Barbara smiled indulgently. "Missy's young, with the blessed obliviousness of inexperience. Parents are cursed with an awareness of reality."

The philosophical observation segued into a prolonged silence. Finally, Richard rose. "I've taken up too much of your lunch hour."

"But you haven't finished your apple," she observed.

Richard looked at the apple, grinned and placed it gently on the edge of her desk. "I couldn't take an apple away from a teacher."

Barbara knew she should say something clever or, at the very least, coherent. But suddenly Richard was looking at her in a way that unleashed a flood of memories and she was too overwhelmed to speak.

"This is insane," he said, the three words packed with frustration. "I've got to see you. Not here. Somewhere where we can talk."

She nodded.

"Tonight? I'll take you to dinner."

"Come to my apartment," she said. "We'll be more comfortable there. I'll make dinner."

He smiled nostalgically. "Do you still make those brownies?"

"I haven't made them in years," she confessed. "But I've still got the recipe."

She stopped at the supermarket for cocoa and nuts for the brownies on her way home from work. She also stopped at the drugstore.

This time, it wasn't mascara she bought.

# 3

THE BROWNIES were cooling on a rack on the kitchen counter. The potatoes were wrapped in paper towels, ready for the microwave. The chicken breasts were marinating.

Barbara was also marinating—in scented water in the bathtub. After the frantic orgy of shopping, cooking and cleaning, she had allotted herself fifteen minutes to relax, and let go of the anxiety that had had her tied up in knots ever since she'd recognized Richard's voice on the telephone.

The deep breaths she took in were renewing and the tepid water leeched surface tension from her muscles, but nothing could still the turmoil in her mind.

*Richard Benson was coming to dinner. She'd made him brownies.* It was as if seventeen years had dissipated in a poof! She was feeling the same giddy, butterflies-in-the stomach exhilaration she'd always felt when she thought of Richard, experiencing the same sense of euphoria she'd always experienced while waiting for him to come over to see her. She'd even gotten the same warm, fuzzy feeling she'd always gotten from making him the brownies she knew he loved.

She reminded herself that she was not a seventeen-year-old with no responsibilities anymore. She was a thirty-four-year-old guidance counselor. And Richard wasn't a suave college man. He was a very troubled father of a pregnant teenager in desperate need of female support.

A languid sigh pushed through her lips as she rested her neck on the rim of the tub. Why couldn't she have bumped into him at the supermarket? At the zoo? He sold real estate—why couldn't she have encountered him when she was trying to buy a house?

*Richard.* His face danced in her mind as she closed her eyes, drew in a deep breath, held it, then released it slowly. He was so much the same, yet so different: mature and confident, yet desperately concerned over his daughter.

His daughter. Missy. Dear, sweet, vulnerable Missy, who'd decided Barbara would be an easy person to talk to.

Barbara groaned, hoping she didn't live to rue her decision to counsel the girl. True, Missy wasn't unbalanced; she was just desperately in need of female companionship. And Barbara had a soft spot as big as a crater for children in need of love or attention. But was it wise to become so involved with Richard's daughter?

*Richard's daughter.* How strange life was at times. Richard had been given a child he hadn't planned when he was ill-prepared for a child, while Barbara had been denied children of her own. Now she was being drawn into Missy's life in the intimate role of friend and confidante.

It probably wasn't wise to become involved with Richard's daughter, but the wisdom, or lack thereof, of becoming involved had not been a factor in her decision to counsel Missy. She would have helped any student in need of her help. The fact that Missy was Richard's child only made her more precious to Barbara. If things had happened differently—

Barbara forced the thought aside. What good were ifs and might-have-beens? She'd put the hurt of Richard's betrayal behind her and gone on with her life a long time ago.

She just hadn't realized that, although she'd set aside the hurt and betrayal, her affection for Richard had remained intact, scrunched unobtrusively in a corner of her heart, waiting for the mention of his name, the sound of his voice and the sight of his face to bring it back to life. She did not remember the hurt or the betrayal when she looked at Richard's face; she remembered the scent of honeysuckle flavoring the air on warm summer nights, the sound of his laughter, the way his eyes crinkled when he smiled, the hardness of his chest under her cheek as they danced to slow, sentimental songs.

Reluctantly she let the water out of the tub and dried herself with a towel. Richard would be here soon, and she wanted to look good. Not conspicuously good, as though she'd made a special effort, but good. After much deliberation, she decided on charcoal jeans and an oversize coral turtleneck. The jeans fit her perfectly; the coral was a flattering color for her, and the silver puffed-heart pendant on a long chain that her parents had given her for her birthday added an elegant touch to the stark simplicity of the sweater. A touch of color on her cheeks, an extra fluff of her hair and she was as ready as she was ever going to be to greet Richard.

She arranged the brownies on a serving plate and set the table, fussing with the place mats and napkin holders until the doorbell signaled Richard's arrival. She forced herself to walk to the door slowly.

He'd brought flowers, a mixed bouquet wrapped in colored cellophane and tied with a ribbon. He offered them to her sheepishly. "I wasn't sure you'd like wine."

"They're pretty," she said, lifting them to smell one of several pink roses in the bouquet. "Thank you."

He followed her to the kitchen and watched as she unwrapped the flowers and put them in a vase. His presence in the small room unnerved her, and she fussed with the flowers unnecessarily before giving them a final pat of approval.

Immediately she shifted her attention to the potatoes, checking to be sure they were snugly wrapped before putting them into the microwave oven and setting the temperature control and timer. She smiled awkwardly before picking up a pot holder and opening the oven door.

A cloud of fragrant steam wafted from the interior as she pulled out the rack and, using a large spoon, basted the sizzling chicken breasts with marinade before sliding the rack back into place, closing the door and replacing the spoon in the ceramic spoon rest on the stove top.

"You always were a good cook," Richard said.

"I don't think nuking potatoes in a microwave and baking chicken qualifies me as a gourmet," she said, grinning. "By the way, would you like something to drink to wash down that brownie you just snitched? Milk?"

"What?" he asked, unable to suppress a smile as he brought his right hand around from behind his back, letting her see the brownie he'd been hiding. "No lecture about ruining my appetite?"

"I'm not your mother," she said, reaching into the refrigerator for the milk carton. "Besides, I don't recall anything ever spoiling your appetite."

Richard took a hefty bite of brownie, closed his eyes as he concentrated on the taste of the rich chocolate, then sighed ecstatically. "They're as good as I remembered."

*And not just the brownies,* he thought as he chased the brownie with a draft of milk from the glass Barbara handed him. Milk and brownies . . . and Barbara. Her face, her voice, her unpretentiousness and generosity carried him back to a time when everything had been simpler, before one foolish mistake had turned everything upside down.

He'd spent seventeen years regretting that youthful error in judgment, trying to recover from the fallout of his macho stunt. Seventeen years! Fatherhood. A wife who couldn't adapt to marriage or motherhood. His mother's ill-concealed contempt. The struggle to keep afloat financially. Guilt over all the people he'd hurt and disappointed, himself included. And Barbara.

He'd lived a long time with the memory of the hurt on Barbara's face when she'd seen him walk into the stadium with Christine hanging on his arm. There had been no satisfaction in that hurt expression, not even a momentary sensation of triumph. There had only been the sudden certainty that he was making a horrible mistake and the even more humiliating realization that he hadn't wanted to stop what he'd started. Christine had snuggled up to him with sex on her mind, and Barbara—Barbara with the big doe eyes filled with hurt—had been the one who'd pushed him away. He remembered thinking that it was time she grew up and realized what a man needed.

*Man!* He'd been a horny, nineteen-year-old virgin out to prove his virility. But the only thing he'd proved was that he could produce sperm that were strong swimmers.

"These'll be beautiful on the table," Barbara said, carrying the vase of flowers to the small table already set for two.

Richard watched her work, marveling at the familiarity of her gestures and the way she moved. She was a woman now, mature, yet she was the same Barbara he'd known in those days of innocence and frustrated yearning—and just looking at her sent a familiar fire burning through his blood.

The microwave sounded and she scurried past him on her way back to the kitchen. "Time to rotate the potatoes."

Potatoes were supposed to be rotated? Well, that could account for the dried-out, crunchy hand grenades he wound up with when he tried to nuke potatoes in the microwave. He followed her, stood at her elbow as she switched the potato on the left to the right and vice versa, then gave the potatoes half a turn.

"You're supposed to do that? Move them around?" he asked.

"At least once, sometimes twice," she replied. "Otherwise you have spots that are overdone, and spots that are raw."

"Hmm," he replied.

"I'm also lowering the heat."

"Told you you were a good cook."

"I just read the instruction book that came with the microwave."

"They come with instruction books?"

"Usually," Barbara said, amusement in her voice. She spun abruptly, not realizing he was so close, and they collided, chest to chest. She shrieked in surprise, then laughed nervously. "Sorry. I—" she backed up half a step "—I'm not used to anyone else in the kitchen."

*Especially not Richard Benson.* He was just under six feet tall and slender, but he seemed so much larger in the small room. She'd moved back so far that her hips pressed against the cabinet, but she could still feel warmth emanating from him. There was a familiarity about his warmth, like the taste of hot chocolate or the weight of a favorite blanket on a cold night, that was luring and seductive.

For a moment, as their gazes locked, she sensed that he was feeling the same seductive pull. His smile was tinged with reluctance as he lifted an eyebrow and said drolly, "I'll, uh, just guard the brownies while you cook."

Barbara had to grin as he picked up a second brownie. "I used to wonder if you just pretended to like them to please me," she said.

The sound of his belly laugh, rich and spontaneous, unleashed another wave of memories. "The way you pretended to like *Young Frankenstein* to please me?"

"*Young Frankenstein?* I wasn't pretend—"

His gotcha expression silenced her denial. "We went to see that movie six times—"

"Seven," she corrected.

"Seven times, and you never watched it all the way through. You buried your face against my arm any time it was the least bit scary. And then you'd tell me how funny it was and how much you enjoyed it."

"I knew you loved it, and I didn't want you going to see it with anyone else," she said. "I was afraid if you went with Mike and Tubbs and the rest of your buddies that you'd gawk over Teri Garr's knockers."

Richard burst out laughing. "God, Barbara. Teri Garr's knockers? The only reason I kept taking you back to see it was that when you were hanging onto my arm for dear life, your own knockers were pretty close to my biceps. That was enough to make me forget about *almost* seeing Teri Garr's on the screen."

Barbara felt her face color as she stared at him, astonished. Richard shrugged, also a bit embarrassed by his confession. "I was only eighteen."

Barbara's soft laughter gave him permission to laugh along with her. They'd both been young—almost achingly young.

Another ding of the timer on the microwave drew Barbara's attention back to the potatoes. "Done," she pronounced, after giving each a subtle squeeze. "What do you like on yours?" she asked, taking sour cream, margarine and grated cheese from the refrigerator.

"The works," he said.

Later, after he'd devoured most of the potato and was putting a third chicken breast on his plate, Barbara grinned at him from across the table. "Too bad you weren't hungry."

He ducked his head in a gesture that was at once familiar. "I'd forgotten how good home cooking is. We haven't had much of it at our house since Mom moved out."

"You and Missy—?"

"Never learned to cook." He laughed nervously. "My mother was a bit . . . obsessive. She wouldn't let anyone in the kitchen when she was working."

"So . . . do you eat pizza every night?" Barbara couldn't imagine the scenario he described. One of her earliest memories was of playing "cook" with the leftover biscuit dough after her grandmother had cut biscuits.

"I've mastered noodles that go with bottled sauce, and Missy's gotten to the point where the hamburgers are done inside before they're too crunchy outside. And we bought a microwave last month."

"You didn't have a microwave?"

"According to Missy, we were the last family in America to get one." He grinned sheepishly. "Mother flatly refused to have one in the house. She was convinced they were radioactive."

"Where did your mother go?" Barbara asked. "If you don't mind telling me."

"I don't mind. My uncle had Alzheimer's, and she went to help her sister out when he was in the final stages. He died early last summer, and Mother stayed on to be with my aunt." He took a breath and released it. "They're doing some traveling, spending six weeks in Europe."

"That's great."

Richard hesitated thoughtfully before replying. "It's probably best . . . for everybody."

"Especially for Missy?" Barbara asked incisively.

Richard's gaze locked with hers across the table. "My mother helped with Missy, even before Christine and I...but lately, since Missy began to...since she turned into a young woman—" He sighed. "It was almost a relief when she left."

"And you feel guilty for feeling relieved?" she asked gently.

He frowned at her. "Didn't your mother ever tell you that it's not nice to read peoples' minds?"

"No," she replied, undaunted. "But I'm sure your mother would have been happy to."

Richard's eyes narrowed shrewdly. "There's a point you're trying to make."

She reached across the table to touch his arm. "No relationship is a panacea. You're not discounting all the good things your mother did for Missy when you acknowledge that her particular form of nurturing may not be what Missy needs at this point in her development."

A frown hardened Richard's mouth. "When Missy told me about...her problem...all I could think of was that I was glad Mother wasn't here. I dread telling her. It's going to be like history repeating itself."

*History repeating itself.* Suddenly, to Barbara, the history he referred to didn't seem nearly remote enough. Visions of Richard walking into the stadium with Christine invaded her mind. Embarrassed, she dropped her gaze to the water goblet next to her plate and tried to be nonchalant as she pulled her hand away from his arm to pick up the glass.

Richard felt her sudden withdrawal acutely. Not that he blamed her. Her face, deliberately turned away from his now, wasn't so different from the face she'd turned to his in frozen disbelief seventeen years ago; if her eyes met his, the pain would be there now, just as it had been then.

Guilt, caustic and relentless, gnawed at him. God, wasn't there a statute of limitations on regret? How long did a man have to live with his mistakes, regretting them, before he was granted some measure of pardon? Or peace?

He'd never apologized to her. Until he'd walked into her office yesterday, he hadn't spoken to her since that horrid argument when he'd said such hurtful things. He'd almost called her from the dorm after he'd returned to school, but he'd decided to wait until he could see her in person to straighten things out.

*What if he hadn't waited?* He'd spent a lot of idle moments through the years wondering. Would things have been easier if he'd written a letter or made a call before Christine dropped the bombshell of her pregnancy? Or would it have been even harder? Would he have had the strength to marry Christine if he hadn't believed that Barbara despised him for the way he'd treated her?

"You don't have to finish that," Barbara said, wresting him from deep thought. He looked down and realized he'd been picking at his food.

"I'm not passing up a single bite," he said, although the guilt gnawing at his insides had effectively killed his appetite. He sliced the remaining piece of chicken on his plate into two bite-size pieces, forked one into his mouth, chewed by rote, then followed with the last. With a flourish, he placed his fork across his plate and his napkin beside it.

*What now?* Barbara thought as their eyes met expectantly. She saw the heat seep slowly into his eyes as he studied her face, a slow, sensual burn that set off explosions of awareness and need inside her. She understood the sensations better now. But she was no more immune to them than she had been when she'd been a seventeen-year-old virgin.

She smiled self-consciously, wondering why, when so many men had tried so many more elaborate ploys without success, Richard could make her feel this way so simply. A smile and a look, and she was burning inside.

"So," she said, standing and gathering dishes to take to the kitchen, "tell me what you've been up to in the past seventeen years."

Richard rose and gathered more of the paraphernalia from the meal. "I'll fill you in while I do the dishes."

"You're my guest. You don't have to—"

"It's the least I can do. You cooked."

Barbara grinned. "When it comes to washing dishes, I'm easily persuaded." She pointed out the disposal, the sink stopper and the dishwasher, then proceeded to wrap leftovers and put away the salad dressing and margarine.

"How about some coffee?" she suggested. "It's early, but I have decaf if—"

"I'll take it straight," he said.

She quickly measured coffee into the coffeemaker and added water, then leaned against the counter and watched him load the dishwasher, much as he'd watched her cook earlier. "You're supposed to be telling me the story of your life for the past seventeen years," she said.

"There's really not that much to tell," he said. "You've seen Missy. Officially, my marriage to Christine lasted three years, but it was over long before that. My mother helped with Missy until last year. That's about it."

"Not quite," Barbara said. "The last time I heard about you, you'd dropped out of college. Now you're a successful real estate broker, with your own office."

Richard paused before replying. "I tried a lot of jobs to keep things going. The ones that paid well were dirty and hard. The ones I liked didn't pay. And there were quite a few that I didn't like and that were dirty and hard and didn't pay worth a damn, to boot."

He stared down at his wet hands in sad reflection. "I was working at a hardware store and one of our customers took a shine to me. He asked if I'd ever thought of going into sales."

He grinned. "He seemed to think I was personable. I wasn't even sure what it meant. But when he asked if I wanted to hang around his real estate office to see if I thought it might be something I might like to do, I took him up on the offer. Hell, it sounded better than selling nails and telling people how to change ball cocks in their toilets. And it was."

"And you were good at it."

"My timing was fortuitous," he demurred. "We were in a boom situation. You didn't have to be good to succeed, you just had to be adequate. And if you were better than adequate, you did very well."

"You shouldn't be so reticent about taking credit where credit's due," Barbara said. "You must have been better than adequate to end up with your own business."

Meeting her gaze, he smiled sadly. "You always did focus on the best in people."

"Maybe that's why I became a guidance counselor."

"I don't know why I was so surprised to see you in that office. When I think about it, it was the most logical place in the world for you to end up."

She gave him a skeptical look. "In a counselor's office, maybe. In the school where your daughter is a student—it was a bit of a long shot. Especially when you consider that we're hundreds of miles from where we grew up."

"I followed the booming real estate market. How did you end up here?"

"New neighborhoods, new schools. Mrs. Stephon was my supervising teacher when I did my student teaching. When she was recruited to be principal here and started putting together her team, she called and asked if I'd like to apply. I loved the area when I came to interview, and I took the job when they offered it. So . . . *voilà!*"

Richard, finished with the dishes, was drying his hands. He grinned suddenly.

"What is it?" she asked.

"I remember when you learned that word."

Barbara grinned back at him. "Oh, yes. First year French. I thought I was terribly sophisticated." She waved her hand in the air and affected a Continental air. *"Voici! Voilà!"*

His grin grew into a full-fledged smile. "The twittering of the birds."

She laughed softly. *"Le gazouillement des oiseaux.* You never did learn to say it in French."

"I never wanted to. I just liked hearing you say it. It sounded sexy."

Barbara shook her head. "What did we know about sexy? We were kids."

"Hormones," he said humorlessly, thinking that perhaps he'd known more about what was sexy and what was good at eighteen than he had known at nineteen or anytime since. Seeing Barbara now and remembering what he'd felt for her was proof enough.

The conversation had turned dangerous. The mechanical click of the coffeemaker automatically shutting off sounded loud in the silence that had descended over the small room. "The coffee's ready," Barbara said, relieved to have something to focus on.

She filled the mugs she'd set out. "Why don't we take it into the living room?"

Richard sat down in one of the overstuffed armchairs flanking the sofa. Barbara handed him a mug, and placed the second mug on the coffee table in front of the sofa. She took a long route to the sofa, detouring in front of the stereo in the entertainment system. "I have a new tape of oldies from the seventies. Want to try it?"

"Sure."

"It's humiliating when the music that was popular when you were a kid turns up on an oldies collection," she said, peeling the cellophane wrapping from the tape. She slid the cassette into the player and adjusted the volume when a Bee Gees' disco number blared through the speakers.

"Tell me about it," Richard said. "I heard a trivia question on the radio the other day, and the answer was Peter Frampton."

"Do you think that means we're getting old?"

*Getting old?* He'd just encountered the woman whose heart he'd broken when she was the age of his daughter—his pregnant daughter—and she wondered if he thought they were getting old?

"It could be a symptom," he said, watching her kick off her shoes and curl her legs under her before reaching for her coffee. She'd always done that, kicked off her shoes and curled up when she was ready to talk.

Silence, laced by the softly playing stereo and memories of shared moments in simpler days, stretched between them as they sipped their coffee. Finally, Barbara set her mug aside. "I was thinking that Missy might come over after school one afternoon a week. We'll just . . . visit and talk about girl stuff."

"In your home? That's very generous of you, but—"

"She'll be more comfortable here than in my office."

Richard nodded uncomfortably. "I'm sure she would. But . . . it just seems like a lot to ask of you."

"Personal interaction with students is the most fulfilling aspect of my job."

"Inviting a student into your home goes a little beyond your job description."

Barbara shrugged. "It's not without precedent for a teacher to take a special interest in a student. She needs a friend, Richard."

Richard exhaled a weary sigh, then looked directly at Barbara. "I know Missy needs a friend. And I know I'm putting her in good hands. I just hate imposing on your generosity."

"She's my student," Barbara said, meeting his troubled gaze levelly. Their eyes remained locked during a long silence before she added softly, "She's your daughter, Richard. Do you think I could refuse to help her if it's within my power to do so?"

Another very long silence ensued before Richard replied, "No, Barbara. I don't think you could ever refuse to help anyone in need. What I can't figure is how you can look at me without wanting to scratch my eyes out for the way I treated you."

Barbara swallowed. "I won't deny that you hurt me. You ripped my heart out and tore it into tiny pieces. But when I remember you, I can't remember one fight and ignore the happy times we shared."

Richard closed his eyes as a look of pure anguish contorted his handsome features. Softly, but with almost explosive intensity, he muttered an expletive.

Opening his eyes, he released a sigh that sounded like a tire going flat. "For the record, I'm sorry I hurt you.

That wasn't what I was trying to do. I just . . . I was try-ing—"

Barbara's smile was bittersweet. "You were trying to grow up."

"I was stupid."

"You made a stupid mistake. Everyone makes stupid mistakes growing up."

"Not the kind I made." *The kind you have to live with for the rest of your life.*

"Not that particular mistake." *But we all have the private demons of our past mistakes.*

Richard picked up his coffee mug and looked inside as though he half expected it to have miraculously re-filled itself, then, finding it empty, put it down again.

"There's plenty in the pot yet," Barbara said, drop-ping her feet to the floor, ready to get it for him.

Richard abandoned the mug and stood. "No. I have to go."

"I wrapped up some brownies for you to take with you. I'll get them," Barbara said.

He watched her scurry to the kitchen. From the back, she appeared as young as her students in her jeans and sweater and with her hair loose around her shoulders. She returned with a paper lunch sack, which she gave to him.

"How do I explain these to Missy?" he asked.

"She didn't know you were coming here?"

He shook his head. "I just said I was going out for a while. She probably assumed I had a house to show. It's not unusual for me to do evening showings."

Barbara winked and grinned conspiratorially. "Maybe you could just sneak them to your office and have them with your morning coffee."

Richard fought to keep his breathing normal. He had a dizzying sense of the years since he'd last seen her falling away. He found it difficult to concentrate on what she was saying when the sight of her face was so distracting.

"Did you tell her that we knew each other?" she asked.

"Hmm?"

"Missy. Did you tell her that we were friends?"

"No. I was so stunned myself. I couldn't see any reason to go into it."

"We have to tell her something," Barbara said. "We don't have to tell her how close we were, only that we knew each other in school. One of those ha-ha, small-world coincidences. Then if one of us should inadvertently mention knowing each other, she won't feel that we deceived her."

Richard nodded absently, distracted by her eyes and the movement of her lips as she spoke.

"I'll send for her tomorrow so we can work out a time for her visits," Barbara continued.

And then, suddenly, a new song started on the stereo. A familiar song. A song they'd hummed along with as it had played on the radio in Richard's Mustang. A song they'd danced to. A song they'd—

"I didn't plan this," Barbara said. "I didn't even know this song was—"

Planned or not, it was too late to stop. Too late to stop the song, too late to stop the memories, too late to stop his arms from sliding around her, his lips from covering hers. Too late to stop herself from feeling the same thrilling magic that only total sensual affinity between two people could generate.

The moment his lips touched hers, she knew that what he'd made her feel before hadn't been a function of youth or innocence; it was the same now, just as urgent and just as thrilling, but richer for their maturity and lack of innocence. Before it had been passion and wonder, and now it was both of those and more that flamed between them.

They were old enough now to understand it. They were old enough to act on it. They would never, Barbara thought with one last shred of logic before she yielded completely to his sensual onslaught, be able to deny it.

And why would they? Why would she be crazy enough to turn away from it twice?

She slid her arms around his waist and pulled him closer. Her hands spread over his back, absorbing the male strength of his body. Her mouth opened under his, accepting him, inviting intimacy.

He filled her senses, all of them. His warmth, his strength, the scent of him, the taste of him, the animal sound of passion he made as he plundered her mouth combined to take her breath and mind away. She didn't care; she didn't want to breathe, didn't want to think. She wanted Richard to make love to her.

When he pulled away from her, it was a physical wrenching. He actually had to pry her arms from around him. "Barbara. We can't do this, Barbara."

*Not do it?* It was incomprehensible. She hadn't felt this way in seventeen years—and she'd been waiting every moment since then to feel this way again. How could he push her away after they'd found each other again? How could he think of not finishing what had been left unfinished for almost two decades?

The betrayal pierced her sharply. She searched his face for answers, finding only a reflection of her own agony, then smoothed her sweater with shaking fingers, as though putting the knit straight would make everything all right. "Are you . . . involved with someone else?" she asked hoarsely.

He shook his head. "No. It's not that simple."

"Then why?" she asked, filling the question with anguish.

Richard couldn't look at her. He closed his eyes and a cry of misery rose from deep inside him to emerge as a groan. He covered his face with his hands and drew in a breath. "I can't explain," he said. "It's not that I don't want you. I ache from wanting you. I've been aching with it ever since I walked into your office."

"Then tell me why!" she said, venting her frustration. "We're not kids anymore. We're responsible adults. We'd be . . . careful. Who would we be hurting if we gave each other pleasure? Just tell me that much. Who would we be hurting?"

The song was still playing—the song they'd danced to, hummed along with—mocking them with the very emotions it stirred in them.

His hands encircled the tops of her arms, as if he felt he had to hold her away from him to prevent her from getting too close. "God, Barbara. I can't think when I'm standing here looking at you like this. I can't talk to you. I can't explain."

"I'm not asking you to talk, or explain. Only to make love to me."

"If I stay half a minute longer, I'm going to," he said intensely, dropping his hands as though afraid his very touch might hurt her. "And then we'd both be sorry."

"Leave, then," she said, whirling away from him. She couldn't look at him; she'd never be able to face him again.

He was across the room, reaching for the doorknob to let himself out, before she added with deceptive calm, "I thought you'd grown up, Richard. I thought you'd learned from your mistakes. But I can see now that was wishful thinking. You're still as self-centered as you were that day you left me for Christine."

He looked as if he might speak. She sensed her name on his tongue, but he never gave it voice. He merely shook his head, squared his sagging shoulders and summoned enough strength to walk through the door.

# 4

AT FIRST, Barbara couldn't move. Cold, empty and aching, she stood in the middle of the room with the disoriented detachment of a disaster victim.

Gradually, though, reality insinuated itself into her conscious awareness. The mellow, seductive song on the stereo ended and was replaced by a ludicrously upbeat disco number with inane lyrics. Barbara stomped to the entertainment center and slapped off the switch.

The resultant silence offered little solace but, rather, seemed to close in around her. She went to the sofa and dropped onto it. Hugging her knees to her chest, she rocked back and forth, sobbing silently and tearlessly as reaction set in.

He had rejected her again. *Richard* . . . had rejected her again. At seventeen, she'd had the resiliency of youth with which to deal with his defection. He'd had the excuse of immaturity for his actions. What was left to her at thirty-five, except humiliation? At thirty-seven, Richard needed no excuse beyond lack of interest.

Barbara ached. She ached physically with sexual frustration, she ached emotionally with embarrassment. Her soul ached with disappointment. So many years she'd wondered, imagined, fantasized, hoped; in all those years, she'd never let go of the dream of what it would be like to have Richard make love to her. Perhaps it was an adolescent fantasy, fated to be shattered. That didn't matter. She'd held on to it with the ferocity of a woman who needed to believe that the joining of two people could be—

She wasn't even sure what she had wanted it to be— just something more than what she'd known. Something like the fulfillment of the promises in those long-ago kisses laced with innocence and passion. She'd thought she and Richard had been granted the chance to find out if their lovemaking could be as special as those kisses.

She picked up a throw pillow and hugged it to her breasts, while an anguished sob broke in her throat. Had it been so wrong for her to hold on to that dream? Had Richard held on to even a piece of it? For a few minutes tonight, when he was kissing her, when his arms were around her, she'd thought—

With all her might, she thrust the pillow across the room. She'd been a fool in every sense of the word, and now she'd have to live with that. But she was bound to see him again, sooner or later; her involvement with his daughter guaranteed it. God, how would she ever look him in the eye and act as if this evening hadn't happened? She found out much sooner than she anticipated, in a most unexpected place. And she flubbed it badly.

She had just arrived at the gym for a basketball game—*the* game, against Lake High's arch rival and major contender for the district title—and stopped at the refreshment stand in the foyer before going into the gym to look for Susan Tanner, who taught biology. Susan was married to the head basketball coach, so she felt duty bound to attend all the games and, whenever possible, she cajoled Barbara into meeting her there.

Carrying a jumbo pretzel in one hand and a soda in the other, Barbara left the vendor's window and headed for the gym, where the pom-pom girls were performing a pregame routine. Later she would curse the impulse that made her turn back for a napkin, for when she turned, she caught sight of Richard at the counter where condiments for the hot dogs sold at the concession stand were kept.

He was not alone. With him was a very attractive Latino woman, with a luxuriant mass of thick, dark hair, vibrant brown eyes, and the warm brown skin tone that women spent hours on the beach or in tanning salons trying to achieve. She was wearing a Lake High T-shirt identical to Barbara's, tucked into a pair of khaki walking shorts. Her breasts were full, her waist minuscule and her legs as well toned as a marathon runner's. Just looking at her made Barbara feel drab and flabby.

The woman spoke animatedly to Richard as she opened plastic packets of mustard and relish and emptied them atop two hot dogs on the counter in front of her. Barbara tried to turn away, ignore his presence, forget she'd seen him at all. But just as she moved to do so, Richard said something back to the woman, and they laughed.

Barbara stared. She knew she was staring, but paralyzed by memories of seeing him with a different woman—a girl, really—at a different game, in a different city, she just stood and stared, feeling again the pain and betrayal of that night half a lifetime ago.

It seemed so fresh and so immediate—how could it still hurt after so many years?

*Because not twenty-four hours ago he walked out of your living room; you offered yourself to him, and he left.* She willed her head to turn, her eyes to look away, her legs to move, but she was too late. He'd spied her. He met and held her gaze, said something to the dark-haired woman and strode toward Barbara in purposeful strides.

Only a full sprint would have enabled her to get away from him, and a full sprint through the thickening crowd of students, parents and faculty would certainly cause a scene and, ultimately, generate gossip. Still, she had to fight off the instinctive, self-preserving response to flee at full speed. Though she took a few steps in a futile attempt to avoid a confrontation, he caught up with her quickly and reflexively reached for her upper arm to stop her.

Not wanting to risk a scene, she stopped. "It's not what it looks like, Barbara. She's a neighbor, a friend. We're not—"

"Don't explain anything to me, Richard. It's none of my business who you're with, and I really couldn't care less."

"That wasn't what the expression in your eyes said," Richard replied.

"That was—" She ducked her head, unable to face him. She swallowed, and started over. "That was just a momentary sense of déjà vu."

"I wouldn't hurt you for anything in the world."

"Richard, please," she pleaded.

Richard shifted his weight restlessly. "Missy told me she talked to you."

Without looking at his face, Barbara nodded.

"You and she decided on a day for her to visit."

"Tuesday," Barbara confirmed on the front end of a sigh. She wished she hadn't agreed to counsel his daughter, even informally. As much as she wanted to be objective, she wasn't sure she could. And if she botched everything, Missy was the one who stood to get hurt most.

"She's looking forward to—"

Richard was interrupted by the summons of the woman at the counter. "Rick!"

When he looked in her direction, she held up the hot dogs and shrugged her shoulders apologetically. "I've got to get into the concession stand. The popcorn machine—"

He turned back to Barbara. "I've got to go," he said with obvious regret. "Maybe we could—?"

"I don't think so," Barbara said, seizing the opportunity to escape and wanting to be lost in the crowd before he could retrieve his hot dogs and come after her.

She found Susan and spent the first quarter of the game worrying that Richard might find her. But by the middle of the second quarter, she'd relaxed enough to become involved in the fast-moving game. Lake fell behind by two points, caught up and fell behind again. With less than a minute left in the half, the team's starting center, Eddie Munoz, landed a tying basket.

The cheerleaders grew red-cheeked with excitement and the crowd of home team supporters exploded with cheers of encouragement. Eddie followed up with another two baskets in rapid succession, giving Lake a four-point lead at the half. The band exploded into the school's fight song as the players left the court.

"What a game!" Susan said. "Roger's going to be so wound up he won't be able to sleep until Sunday." Grinning naughtily, she added, "Unless I relax him."

"You're hopeless," Barbara said.

"Nope. Just horny," Susan said. "I swear, Roger gets so worked up when they're practicing for a big game that he forgets what his husbandly duty is."

"I'm sure you remind him."

"I don't have a drawerful of see-through teddies for nothing," Susan said.

"They're playing great tonight," Barbara said.

"Yeah. Especially Eddie Munoz. He's trying extra hard since his dad got to come to the game. They weren't sure they'd be able to get him here. That's him in the wheelchair behind the bench." She offered Barbara her field glasses.

"What's wrong with him?" Barbara asked, accepting the binoculars.

"You haven't heard about it? It's the weirdest thing. An old war wound, from Vietnam. Last month he was mowing and pulled on the lawn mower and fell down, paralyzed. They X-rayed him and there was a piece of shrapnel pressing into his spine. It's been inside him all these years and gradually shifted."

"How awful!" Barbara said. "Is the paralysis permanent?"

"It's a wait-and-see. They removed it, but they don't know exactly how much damage it did. They won't know for a while, but he's getting some feeling back in his feet, which is a hopeful sign."

The pom-pom girls were on the court, dancing and shaking their pom-poms to an upbeat song from the band. Barbara looked beyond them to the wheelchair parked between the team bench and the first row of bleacher seats. "He's a big man," she observed absently.

"Six-six," Susan confirmed. "He was a scholarship player in college basketball. His size is part of the problem. It's a nightmare getting him anywhere. Can you imagine trying to lift him?"

"That's rough," Barbara said. Succumbing to lurid curiosity, she raised the field glasses for a closer look at Mr. Munoz.

"Eddie's a big kid, but he can't get him in and out of the chair without help," Susan continued. "If it weren't for one of their neighbors, I guess he wouldn't get out at all."

Too caught up in what she was watching, Barbara grunted noncommittally. Munoz's helpful neighbor had just moved within range of the field glasses, smiling affably as he handed Munoz a soda and said something that made them both laugh. Barbara knew what the neighbor's laughter would sound like, because the neighbor's face was as familiar to her as her own reflection in the mirror. And so was the tenderness in the neighbor's eyes—a tenderness discernible even through binoculars across a gym.

"Hey, what's so interesting over there?"

Barbara lowered the glasses. "Nothing! I—I was just looking at Mr. Munoz." She forced a smile. "Just morbid curiosity."

Susan frowned skeptically but didn't comment. The moment was saved from awkwardness when the cheerleaders led the team back onto the court and the crowd broke into a raucous cheer. Lake built their slight lead to a comfortable eight points by the end of the third quarter and won by twelve.

"Roger should be in a good mood tonight," Barbara said as the fans began leaving the bleachers. "The boys played well."

"As if you noticed!" Susan said. "Why do I get the feeling your mind wasn't on basketball tonight?"

"My mind's never on basketball," Barbara countered. "You know I only come to the games to humor you."

"Well, you seemed particularly disinterested tonight. Listen, Roger won't be home for at least a couple of hours. Why don't we go get a pizza or something and you can tell me why you were so distracted."

"Not tonight," Barbara said. "It's been a rough week, and I'm a little tired. Besides," she added with a grin, "you need plenty of time to pick out a teddy."

"No decision to be made on game nights," Susan said. "When the team wins, I wear the school colors. When they lose, I wear black."

Barbara shook her head. "Like I said, you're hopeless."

They walked together as far as the foyer, speaking to several students along the way. Then they ran into a couple of other teachers who asked Susan to pass along their praise to her husband for the team's fine performance. At length the conversation worked its way to the suggestion of a victory celebration. Barbara gave Susan's elbow a squeeze. "You go ahead. I'm going to cut out. I'll see you Monday."

Her timing couldn't have been worse, for as she walked through the parking lot, her attention was drawn to a commotion a few cars away from hers. She recognized Richard's voice above the din. "All right, now. Ready? On three."

Several other voices joined his to form a chorus. "One—two—three."

"Lift!" Richard said, and then, straining, added, "No more hot dogs for you, Munoz. You're as heavy as a heifer."

With the help of another man, he was heaving the paralyzed man into the front seat of a sedan.

"Watch his head!" This from Mrs. Munoz, who was hovering anxiously, supervising the transfer.

"You couldn't hurt a head this hard with a sledgehammer," Richard said, then asked Munoz playfully, "How do you put up with this woman's nagging?"

Munoz, safely in the front seat, laughed. "She's got great legs."

The nag with the great legs was attempting to fold the wheelchair, struggling with one of the adjustments.

"Need some help?" Richard offered.

"This clamp is always stubborn."

"I'll get it," Richard said, taking over the task.

Barbara used his moment of preoccupation to hurry to her car, and drove away from the parking lot without a backward glance.

But not, alas, without a backward thought. This latest encounter with Richard had left her shaken. She'd been foolish enough last night, throwing herself at Richard and inviting his devastating rejection of her. Tonight her reaction to seeing him with another woman had been downright bizarre.

It was more than déjà vu, more than just the feeling of having been in that situation before. Tonight, Barbara had actually relived that horrid moment when she'd seen Richard with Christine. She had felt the same pain, the same betrayal.

Once home, she kicked off her shoes, then released her hair from the barrette holding it in a ponytail at her nape. She combed her fingers through the loose hair. The familiarity of her apartment was soothing, but not soothing enough to convince her that she wasn't coming unhinged where Richard was concerned.

Though weary, she knew she wouldn't be able to sleep so early. Nor would she be able to concentrate well enough to read. So she curled up on the couch, turned on the television and flipped from a sitcom to an investigative news show to a stand-up comedy special before finally returning to the news show.

She had the vague notion that she should pay attention to the reporter exposing waste in government spending. Sooner or later the price paid by the government for eraser-tip pencils was bound to work its way into the conversation in the teachers' lounge.

During the station break, she rummaged in the kitchen for something to eat, then settled back in front of the TV set with a glass of juice and a brownie.

The exposé on government waste had yielded to the exploration of an often-overlooked, frequently mis-diagnosed, little understood disease. Barbara nibbled at the brownie as she listened to sufferers describe the anguish of having a disease no one understood and thought, with uncharacteristic indulgence in self-pity, that anguish was not limited to sufferers of oddball diseases. On top of having made a fool of herself and being rejected, she was probably going to gain two pounds on the brownies she'd made for Richard.

The doorbell surprised her. At half-past ten? Think-ing it was probably a neighbor with some minor crisis, she was more cautious than alarmed, but glad she had a peephole so she could check out who was at the door before opening it.

After seeing the face of her unexpected caller, she wished she hadn't looked. Just what did Richard think he was going to accomplish by showing up on her doorstep unannounced this late at night? Whatever it was, she didn't need the grief. Though she'd seen him, he hadn't seen her. And she was going to keep it that way.

She tiptoed back to the sofa and curled up in the cor-ner, hugging her legs, intent on ignoring the doorbell.

Another ring. In the apartment next door, her neighbor's yappy little dog, Gizmo, barked hysteri-cally. Barbara buried her face against her knees and groaned softly. *Please, oh, please, Richard—just go away!*

But he didn't go away. He waited a reasonable inter-val, then rang again. And knocked. "Barbara? I can hear your television. I know you're in there."

Gizmo went wild, and Barbara groaned again. She should have known ignoring him wouldn't work. Feeling wooden, she switched off the television and walked to the door. Still, she hesitated, not finding the strength to reach for the knob.

She leapt when the bell sounded again, then, with a grim shrug, opened the door with the chain lock still engaged and spoke through the narrow opening. "Go away, Richard."

"I need to talk to you."

"It's late." Gizmo was in a frenzy, zipping and scratching at his door.

"I want to explain about last night," Richard persisted.

"I didn't need any explanations when I was seventeen. I certainly don't need any at thirty-four."

"You've got it all wrong, Barbara."

The door next to Barbara's opened an inch, and Gizmo's nose pressed through. His owner's eye also appeared and gave Richard a critical once-over. "Are you all right, Barbara?"

Barbara sighed dismally. "Yes, Carolyn," she replied. "It's all right. I know this man."

Gizmo clawed at the ground. "Humph," Carolyn said skeptically.

Barbara shrugged, and closed her door far enough to disengage the chain. "He was just coming inside."

Pinning Richard with another look—as though memorizing features for a police report—Carolyn said, "Well—"

"It's all right, Carolyn," Barbara said emphatically, giving Richard an even more pointed look than Carolyn had. "Trust me, I know this man. He's not going to try anything."

"You didn't have to say that," Richard said once they were in the living room.

"Carolyn was concerned," Barbara countered. "I don't get many male visitors this late at night. I thought I'd put her mind at rest. And it's not as though I have to worry about your jumping my bones, is it?"

"Barbara, please. Don't. You got it all wrong. It had nothing to do with you."

Barbara's humorless laugh bordered on hysteria. "We kissed. I asked you to stay. You left. What's to get wrong?"

"Barbara," he said, and cringed as she winced. She didn't want to talk to him, didn't want to hear anything he had to say, didn't want him in her home. He didn't blame her, after what had almost happened between them and the way he'd bolted.

He hadn't meant to hurt her, but that didn't excuse the fact that he had. From the way he'd reacted when he found her in that office, he should have had better sense than to trust himself alone with her, but he'd been greedy for all the things she represented to him.

"It was five minutes of insanity," she said, clinging to control with the most tenuous hold possible. "We listened to an old song and—"

The guarded expression in her eyes tore at Richard's heart as he realized that the wariness was his handiwork.

"Hurting you is the last thing in the world I'd want to do," he said. "I hope you can believe that."

She bowed her head, refusing—perhaps unable—to look at him any longer.

"Why are you here, Richard?" she asked softly, her words laced with profound sadness. "What did you hope to accomplish by coming back here?"

"I couldn't let you think that my . . . hasty departure had anything to do with you."

She chortled incredulously. "Why would I think that? I threw myself at you and you retreated. Nothing personal."

Silence followed, broken finally by Richard's sigh. "You wouldn't have a cup of coffee, would you?"

"Sorry," she said, then offered reluctantly, "I could make hot chocolate."

"I haven't had hot chocolate in—"

"If you say seventeen years, you're a dead man," she snapped.

He grinned sheepishly. "A very long time."

He followed her to the kitchen. Although she had instant mix that required only hot water, she made real cocoa, making a paste of powdered chocolate and sugar and then adding milk. She heated it in a saucepan on the stove, stirring constantly, instead of sticking it into the microwave. Maybe she wanted something to think about besides the discussion that was both imminent and inevitable. Or maybe, despite all reason and self-preservation, despite common sense, she liked having Richard there, liked doing something domestic for him while he watched her work.

Maybe she was just plain crazy, she thought, staring at the swirls her wooden spoon painted in the white froth atop the brown liquid. *Or maybe she loved him,*

*and always would. Even if it made no sense. And even
if it meant she'd be hurt.*

She poured the steaming cocoa into mugs and
handed one to Richard. "I, uh, don't have any marshmallows."

"I don't need marshmallows," he said, smiling so
sweetly that Barbara wanted to cry.

They stayed in the small kitchen, Richard leaning
against one end of the counter, Barbara leaning against
the other. Richard took a sip. "This is good."

Barbara set her mug down on the counter, hard. *How
much more of this was she supposed to take?* "We've
already established that I know my way around a
kitchen, Richard. Why don't you just say what you
came to say?"

Richard studied the liquid in his mug for several seconds before setting the mug on the counter with a thud.
His fist followed, dealing a blow that set glass rattling
in the cupboard. "Damn it, Barbara. Why couldn't we
have run into each other last year, or last summer? Why
not three years ago, or three months ago? Why not any
time before—"

Turning his back to her, he slapped both hands on the
countertop in frustration and muttered a curse. Every
line in his body, from his tense stance to his clenched
jaw, suggested misery.

Barbara tentatively approached him and placed a
hand on his shoulder lightly.

A sigh shuddered through him, racking his shoulders under her fingertips. He spun around, leaving
Barbara's hand suspended in midair. She let it drop to
her side as their gazes locked. Never taking his eyes

from her face, Richard lifted his hand and traced the curves of her cheeks with trembling fingertips.

Barbara held her breath as he plunged his fingers into her hair, cradling her scalp.

"Your face," he said. "God, Barbara, you should see it. And your eyes. I wish I could tell you how it makes me feel when I look at you and see you looking up at me. You make me remember what life was like before everything got so screwed up."

Barbara's breath caught in her throat as he caressed the sensitive areas in front of her ears with his thumbs. His expression was primitive and hungry, as though he could devour her, and Barbara's response was equally primitive and intense. He was the only man who'd ever made her feel this way; she thought perhaps he was the only man who ever would or could.

Richard swallowed. "If I keep touching you, I'm going to forget all the reasons I shouldn't."

His hands started to slide away from her head and Barbara stopped them by covering them with her own hands, trapping them. Her eyes locked with his unflinchingly as she rasped, "Touch me."

# 5

RICHARD TENSED and rigidly pulled his hand free. He took several steps back. A strangled sound in his throat was his only reply.

"Then tell me why," Barbara demanded. "Just tell me what all these mysterious reasons you can't touch me are. It's what you came for, isn't it? To explain? Well, I'm listening."

"I can't risk . . . I'm not going to screw up your life, too."

"Too?"

His bitter chortle was ugly. "Haven't you heard? All I have to do is unzip my pants and lives go toppling like bowling pins. Just stand in line and take a number."

"Richard," she said, too taken aback by his virulent self-derision to think of anything more coherent. She had sensed that he was under pressure—understandable for a single father with a pregnant teenage daughter. But this was more. He was tormented. She must have been blind not to see how tormented he was.

She reached out to him, instinctively offering a woman's comfort, but he recoiled from her, holding his hands up in front of him as if defending himself from attack. "You can't have a number, Barbara. I'm not adding anyone else to my list of casualties. Especially not you."

An awkward silence followed. Finally, Barbara picked up her cocoa. "It's silly for us to be standing in here when there are comfortable chairs in the living room." She squeezed past him on her way out of the narrow room. "If you feel like talking, I'm a pretty good listener. We were friends once, you know."

*Friends, but never lovers.* The old pain haunted her. Obviously he didn't want a lover; just as obviously, he needed a friend.

Richard was slow joining her—so slow that she half expected him to walk straight to the door for a clean getaway. But he came in and sat down in the same chair he'd sat in on his last visit. Perched on the edge, he leaned forward and propped his elbows on his knees, cradling the mug of cocoa between his hands.

An awful silence ensued. Curled up on the end of the couch, as she had been earlier, Barbara thought that it would be much easier if he left. The emotional turmoil of having run into him had exacted its toll. She was tired, physically and emotionally. She still ached from wanting him, and his rejection was still wedged in her heart like a dagger.

But he needed a friend. He was tormented and alone, more isolated, in his own way, than his daughter Missy was, and there was no way she could have denied him the offer of friendship. The silence engulfing them was thick with his need to unload the demons of guilt and self-loathing, and Barbara was too tired for subtlety.

"It's not a magic cup of cocoa," she said flatly. "You're not going to find the solutions to any of your problems by studying the foam on top."

Richard looked at her and shrugged.

"Tell me why you feel so responsible for Missy's pregnancy," she said.

Richard hesitated. At length, he released a chortle of bitter laughter. "'Of all the gin joints in all the world.'"

"Of all the guidance offices in all the schools," Barbara paraphrased drolly. "Exactly." Richard forced himself to meet Barbara's gaze. "You're probably the last person I ever expected to be talking to about my daughter's problems."

Barbara shrugged. "You're not talking about your daughter's problems yet. Right now, you're avoiding my question."

Scowling, Richard set his cocoa on the coffee table and turned his full attention on Barbara. "Of course I feel responsible for Missy. I'm her father."

"You're responsible for her well-being," Barbara said. "But even the most conscientious parents can't assume the responsibility—or the guilt—for every action a teenager takes."

"I have every right to feel responsible for this one."

"It's natural to feel that way. It's not easy to accept the idea of children growing up and becoming more independent, but they do, and very quickly. It probably hurts to think of Missy being independent enough to—"

"You can spare me the guidance counselor gibberish," Richard snapped. "You don't know—" Shaking his head, he laughed bitterly. "Of course you don't know. But you're going to. I came back tonight to tell you all about it. I didn't want you to think that my leaving—that I didn't want to stay. I just . . . I couldn't. I couldn't do it to you."

He rose and restlessly paced the small area between the entertainment center and the coffee table. Eventually he stopped in front of the stereo, opened the cassette holder and took out the tape and read sarcastically, "'Sizzlin' Seventies.'"

He turned to face her then, but Barbara wasn't sure he was actually seeing her. "When that song came on and you were right there in front of me, it was like the years just fell away. And then you were in my arms and I forgot everything except what it felt like to hold you."

Abruptly he put the tape back in the cassette holder. "It was like tasting innocence again." He laughed a laughter that was ugly and bitter. "You want to know why I feel responsible for Missy's pregnancy? Because my daughter came to me and asked if I thought girls should have sex with their boyfriends. She trusted me enough to come and ask, and I wasn't sharp enough to realize that it was more than a rhetorical question. So I gave her rhetoric."

He ran his fingers through his hair. "Parental rhetoric. The old party line about how sex should be an expression of love between two people who care about each other."

"That's a very healthy 'party line.'"

"Yeah," he agreed bitterly. "And Missy listened very politely. Then she wanted to know if it was true that guys need sex more than girls. What was I supposed to say to that? I told her that it doesn't mean the same thing to guys that it means to girls, that to them it's just a physical thing, but that girls get more emotionally involved. I impressed on her that she should never feel obligated to have sex just because a boy wanted her to, that she shouldn't let anyone pressure her into doing something she wasn't ready to do."

Again he laughed that bitter, self-deprecating laugh. "Did you have some strange sensation that someone was thinking about you? It wasn't easy for me to look at my daughter and remember my performance as a horny teenager."

Barbara grinned. "You're not the first father to do a little squirming when his daughter started to blossom."

"She asked me how long I had to know a woman before I expected her to have sex with me."

"That's a tough one."

"Tough? This is my baby girl. She's not supposed to know what sex is, much less question me on my personal sexual policies. I was in shock."

"What did you tell her?"

"What do you suppose I told her? I'd just given her the 'meaningful expression between people who care' speech. I told her that I had to know a woman well enough to have developed a special affection for her."

He dropped wearily into the chair, sucked in a deep breath, then released it very slowly. "It wasn't *just* rhetoric, you know," he said defensively. "*Playboy* isn't exactly sending out reporters to cover my social life. I was faithful to Christine when we were married, although, God knows, she had no clue what being faithful meant."

Barbara nodded. Despite how their relationship had ended, Richard—the Richard she'd known—was a decent man. It was not surprising in the least to hear that he would take marriage vows seriously, even if the woman he was married to didn't.

"After we separated," he continued, "I was too busy trying to make a living to get involved with women. Even if I'd had the time, I wouldn't have had the energy. There were a couple of relationships that didn't go anywhere, and then, two years ago, there was one I thought might."

He paused pensively, and frowned. "That was another disaster. Neither Missy nor my mother could stand her. But the point is, I didn't lie to Missy when I told her that I had to know a woman before I got involved."

There was a troubling note of defensiveness in his voice. "Did she accuse you of lying?" Barbara asked.

"Accuse?" He pondered the question before replying bitterly, "No. She never...accused me."

"But you don't think she believed you?"

"Oh, she believed me," he said grimly. "Why wouldn't she, until—" Abruptly he stood and paced again, finally stopping in front of a large framed print on the side wall. As he studied the colorful depiction of a Sunday afternoon park scene, he absently slid his hands into the front pockets of his pants.

Barbara's heart swelled with tenderness. She'd seen him stand just that way so many times when he was thoughtful or troubled. The shape and subtle slope of his shoulders was suddenly painfully familiar. She longed to slide her arms around his waist, nestle her cheek against his hard, smooth back and whisper reassurances to him that everything was all right. But that wasn't the kind of reassurance he wanted from her, so she sat perfectly still, waiting, with an air of patience that she did not actually possess, for him to continue confiding in her.

Several minutes passed before he asked, "Do you remember that ticket I got on the way home from the prom?"

"The one for running a red light?"

"It was a yellow light. I sped up to make it through a yellow light. Everybody speeds up to make it through yellow lights, but the one time I tried it, I got a ticket."

"There was a cop sitting at the corner," Barbara said, wondering why he'd brought up such an innocuous event from so long ago.

"Exactly," he said sarcastically, nodding his head. "There was a cop at the corner. The one time I decided to speed up for a yellow light, there was a cop at the corner. It's a pattern in my life—when I take a chance, I get caught. I make the same mistakes other people make, and I end up paying for them forever."

"Mistakes like Christine?"

He spun to face her. "Most guys have a Christine in their background. But they don't end up married to her. I wasn't the first boy Christine was with by a long count. But I was with her twice, in one weekend—twice, and bingo! Forget college, forget the girl you're really crazy about, you're going to be a daddy."

"That was a long time ago, Richard."

"Yeah, well, I'm good at mistakes. My mistakes usually have long-reaching repercussions."

He dropped into the chair again. "I'm still damned good at mistakes."

"What mistake did Missy catch you making?"

Richard froze. Then, slowly, an eerie smile crept over his features. "The same old one," he said. "History repeating itself. I unzipped my pants again." He laughed bitterly. "As usual, it resulted in disaster."

Barbara encountered a lot of self-loathing in her work with troubled students and parents, but she'd seldom witnessed the degree of torment she sensed in him. His misery was almost palpable.

"It was an agent from another Realtor's office. She sold a house I'd listed, so we met during the negotiations. After the closing, she suggested we go to dinner and celebrate. I—" He shook his head. "I wasn't even that interested in her. I guess I developed a habit of tuning out that possibility with women. But Missy was at a football game, and one of her friends was having a slumber party after the game, and Mother had just left for Aunt Sharon's, so—"

He shifted in the chair. "It was a strange feeling when I realized I didn't have to answer to anybody if I decided to go out to dinner. I was thirty-seven years old, and for the first time in my life, I didn't have to answer to anyone if I decided to go out to dinner with a woman."

"So you went to dinner."

He shrugged. "So I went to dinner. And afterward, she asked to see my atrium."

"Is that anything like wanting to see your art prints?" Barbara asked drolly.

Richard scowled at her. "Don't mock me, Barbara. This is hard enough without trying to be cute. We had talked about atria at dinner and I had told her about the tropical garden my mother had put in."

"Sorry," Barbara said.

Richard accepted the apology with a frown. "It doesn't take Einstein to figure out what happened. I just wish to God I'd had the sense to take her into the bedroom instead of staying in the living room." He ran his hand through his hair and exhaled a shuddering sigh. "Missy came home to get something she'd forgotten—"

"Oh, Richard," Barbara said, struggling for objectivity she didn't feel. "How horrible for you."

"Horrible?" he asked with an ugly chortle. "My baby girl finds me with my pants down on the living room sofa with a casual acquaintance two weeks after I told her that I like to get to know a woman before I have sex with her? Yeah, I guess that qualifies as horrible."

Barbara forced herself to sit perfectly still during the silence that followed. *Oh, Richard, why do I have to be your friend and listener? When I see you so bitter, hurting so badly and looking so alone, I just want to hold you.*

"How did Missy react?" she asked tenderly when it became apparent that he wasn't going to continue without prompting.

Richard stared at the far wall, unseeing. "She said one word. 'Daddy.' And then she ran out of the house." He paused again. His eyes were bright—too bright and wet—and his voice was hoarse with emotion. "To the day I die, I'll never forget that horrible night."

"What about since then, since you've both had a chance to recover from the initial shock?"

"She's never mentioned it."

"And you've never brought it up?" Barbara asked, appalled.

Richard's dismal sigh was almost a groan. "What good would it do? It would have been embarrassing for both of us, and it wouldn't change anything."

"Not change anything? Richard, it must have been just as traumatic for her as it was for you. She probably needs to talk about it as much as you do."

He gave her an incredulous stare. "Need to talk about it? My daughter—and quite possibly one or more of her friends—caught me buck naked with a woman on the living room sofa. The less said, the better. The last thing I want to do is talk about it."

"Well, Missy might be dying to talk about it, but too embarrassed to bring it up. You should find out. She could be confused, or she may be carrying around some heavy-duty unresolved anger."

"Two months later Missy came in and announced she was pregnant. I think that pretty much sums up what she thought of the whole thing."

"You think that Missy got pregnant because she interrupted you with a woman?"

"She *emulated* me!" he said bitterly. "I became her casual sex role model! She thought I'd lied to her. She thought I told her one thing and did another." He faced her evenly. "I swear to God, Barbara, I didn't lie to her. It was an isolated incident. I just . . . got caught."

"I believe you," Barbara said. After a long hesitation, she added softly, "Missy would believe you, too, if you explained what happened to her the way you've explained it to me."

"It's a little late for explanations now," Richard said. "But you see why I can't take a chance on getting caught with my pants down again."

He'd dropped the last piece into a complicated puzzle, but Barbara couldn't quite believe the picture that emerged.

"I can't afford another mistake, Barbara. Not with this situation with Missy."

"I see," Barbara said, thinking she should have felt relief that his rejection of her had not been personal, instead of being so outraged about the poor timing that had brought Richard Blake back into her life just when he'd decided he didn't want to risk an involvement. "You took one chance and had a bad experience and now you've taken a vow of celibacy?"

"Do you blame me?"

Barbara bristled. "I don't have to. You're too busy blaming yourself to need anyone else's disapproval."

"I don't exactly have a lot to be proud of lately."

"You're beating yourself up over some very human mistakes. You're a grown man. You took a woman to dinner and . . . got friendly. It's not as though you were married and cheating on a wife, or as if you knew Missy might come home, and deliberately took a chance on her finding you."

Leaning forward, she rested her hand lightly on his forearm. "Lighten up on yourself, Richard. Please. For Missy's sake, as well as your own. You're using up all your energy regretting things you can't do anything about, and you need that energy to help Missy."

Richard looked down at her hand, wishing the weight and warmth of it didn't feel so natural there, so familiar and comforting. Then he lifted his gaze to her face, and the expression in her eyes turned what had been a simple touch of comfort into something much more complex. Torn, he searched inside himself for the strength to pull away from everything that touch offered, while everything in him yearned to cover her hand with his own and invite her closer to him in every way a woman could get close to a man.

He found the strength—barely—and eased his arm just out of her reach, saying her name firmly.

Barbara jerked her hand back as though she'd been shocked.

After an interval of dreadful silence, she spoke, her voice soft but her words intense. "You're not the only one living with mistakes, Richard."

Richard waited with a sense of impending doom for her to continue. He didn't want to hear that her life had been anything less than wonderful. He would have preferred to hang on to the image of her as the wide-eyed teenager he'd known.

"After we broke up—the way we broke up—I was bound and determined not to let anyone hurt me the way you'd hurt me," she said.

Guilt knotted Richard's gut as he listened. Whatever mistake she was talking about, it bounced back to him. To the way he'd treated her. To his own stupid mistake. The last thing in the world he needed was more guilt piled on his shoulders. He'd known he'd hurt her, but that didn't make coming face-to-face with the demons his actions had spawned any easier.

"I wasn't just careful," Barbara continued, "I was . . . almost compulsive. I wouldn't let anyone get close enough to hurt me, and I wouldn't get close to anyone who threw me off balance. Guys came on to me, but if I felt the least bit out of control, I wasn't interested. I wasn't going to be vulnerable again. And then I met Dennis. Dennis was—"

She paused to gather her thoughts. "Dennis was perfect. He was polite, respectful and mature. I didn't have to worry about losing control with Dennis, because he had enough for the both of us. We didn't make love until our wedding night. We agreed on that early on, and waiting was never a problem, the way it had been when I was dating you."

She allowed herself a bittersweet smile that made Richard want to lunge from his chair and devour her, every inch of her, slowly, appreciating every curve and texture and taste along the way. He wanted inside her as acutely as he had when he was a randy buck who'd never been inside anyone outside of his hormone-driven dreams.

The smile that unintentionally taunted him grew into a gentle burst of self-mocking laughter. "I thought I had it all figured out. We weren't thinking below the waist. Not Dennis and I. We had a mature relationship. What we had was more important than some fleeting chemical interaction. We shared mutual goals and we respected each other."

She looked at him as she smiled this time, with the cunning expression of chums sharing a private joke. "It took me a long time to realize just how empty life can be without passion. I'd assumed that once we were alone and touching that it would be . . . that, well, nature would take over and it would be . . . the way it had been when you and I used to—"

"I'm the last person in the world you should be saying this to," he said, desperate to stop her. But she was strong, and he realized suddenly that she always had been.

"No," she said. "In some funny kind of way, you're the only person I could ever say it to. I've never told anyone else how it was. I guess I was afraid they'd think the problem was in me, that I was incapable of passion. I'm not afraid of that with you—not since you kissed me again."

Her eyes met his. "Do you know what a relief it is to find out that I can be passionate beyond reason? That I didn't imagine the magic? That I'm still capable of letting myself feel it?"

She averted her gaze. "I used to lie awake at night wondering if I'd ever really felt it, or if I had just embellished it in my mind, the way children remember things as bigger and brighter and more wonderful than they really were."

"You weren't just imagining," Richard assured her.

A deep sadness haunted her eyes as she smiled. "I knew that the moment you came into my office. And when you looked at me the way you used to look at me, and then you said you had to see me, I was hoping—" She vented her frustration in a sigh. "God, Richard, just once, I wanted to find out what it would be like."

Richard bolted from the chair. How much was a man expected to endure? He was trying to do what was right, what was decent. "You want to know what it would be like?" he said. "I'll tell you. It would be everything we've missed, everything we lost when I gave in to stupidity. It would be there, a part of us, a part of our lives, a pivotal point that divides our lives into before and after. It would be like piecing all those shattered dreams back together. We wouldn't just walk away from it. We ... *couldn't* just walk away unaffected."

"Don't you think I know that?" Barbara said. "Do you think I didn't know that when I went to the drugstore?"

Richard felt as though he'd been poleaxed in the chest. "God, Barbara! You went to the drugstore? Why would you tell me something like that?"

"I was willing to take the chance," she said.

She wasn't referring to telling him about the drugstore, Richard knew. "Well, I'm not!" he said. "My casualty list is long enough."

She rose and collected the cocoa mugs, then turned to him as though he were an afterthought. "Goodbye, Richard."

"I can't risk hurting you again." The argument sounded as futile as a defense attorney's closing statements after the presentation of condemning physical evidence.

"You've told me what you came here to tell me," she said. "Now leave."

Richard wanted to go, but his feet and legs wouldn't cooperate. "I hurt you once. Look what it led to."

"No one's arguing with you, Richard." She brushed past him, carrying the mugs, the way she would have sidestepped a piece of furniture. "There's nothing else to be said. Just ... go."

She stopped, but didn't turn around. Richard studied her—her hair hanging free, the drape of knit across her narrow shoulders, the fullness of female buttocks outlined by her pants, her bare feet. The desire he felt for her was as familiar as an old love song and as compelling as ageless lust. He saw her beauty and her trust, her strength and her vulnerability, and he wanted her with a yearning that cut through him with the sharpness of an executioner's ax. The knowledge that she was his for the asking only fanned the flames of that desire.

"It's best," he said.

"Probably." The word sounded choked.

If he hadn't been watching her so intently, he might have missed the way she winced, a subtle recoil of her entire body.

He was hurting her by leaving—who could say with absolute certainty that he would hurt her any worse by staying? In desperation, he searched his mind and his conscience for the reasons he felt compelled to walk away from her.

He couldn't remember a single one of them. "Like hell it's best!" he snarled.

# 6

RICHARD'S SHOUTED OATH fed into a sudden silence. Barbara was standing, eerily still, at the entrance to the dining nook with her back to him. He waited for her to move, to speak, to indicate, somehow, that she had understood what he'd said, that she hadn't changed her mind, that she still wanted him to stay with her. But she just stood there, shoulders tense and head rigid, motionless and elegant as a statue.

He stepped behind her, close enough to feel the warmth radiating from her soft woman's flesh and hear the whispered rush of her breathing. He would have spoken, but the questions were too fragile to commit to words. At length, he gingerly positioned his hands on her shoulders and urged her around so he could see her face. And her eyes.

Relief spread through him like an unguent. Soothing. Healing. The years fell away, and with them the guilt and deprivation. He was with Barbara, looking at Barbara's face, peering into Barbara's eyes; the sheer splendor of it filled him to overflowing.

Barbara drew in a ragged breath as Richard caressed her cheek with his fingertips, then released it as his thumb teased across her lips, coaxing them apart. The sweetness of his smile seeped deep inside to soothe old hurts.

"What now?" she rasped, surrendering the privilege of decision to him.

He lowered his head and kissed her gently, almost reverently, but when he moved to slide his arms around her, the mugs she was holding wedged between them. With a half chuckle, he took them from her hands, put them on the counter and then turned back to her with deliberate purpose.

Color rose in her cheeks as he devoured the sight of her. Richard still couldn't quite believe the miracle of walking into an office at his daughter's school and finding Barbara; couldn't believe that after years of being haunted by memories of what it was like to hold her, she was there, solid in his arms, flushed, womanly soft. He couldn't believe that he was capable of feeling again all the healthy and hopeful emotions she had awakened in him.

Smiling seductively, she rested her palms on his chest before slowly sliding them over his shoulders and locking her hands behind his neck, urging his head down.

Just having her hands on his nape was unbelievably erotic. The quickened pulse of his heart dizzied him even as he obligingly lowered his mouth to hers. The kiss burned through his senses like wildfire, volatile and consuming. It had always been that way with Barbara, even when they'd been too inexperienced to realize that kisses were more than just two sets of lips pressed together. She'd turned his world upside down the first time she'd smiled at him, and when he'd finally managed to wangle a kiss, she'd sent him soaring into an adolescent male's heaven.

Seventeen years hadn't changed anything. A couple of kisses and she had him as hot and bothered as a little boy bunny in springtime. And if he didn't do something to slow things down, they were going to wind up doing what little bunnies did in the springtime right there on the kitchen table.

He ended the kiss, but continued holding her. When he opened his eyes and looked at her, she smiled and combed her fingers into his hair. He groaned as her thumbs grazed his ears. "No wonder I went nuts at nineteen."

"Do you still like it when I tickle you behind the ear?" she asked mischievously, performing magic with her forefingers.

Richard cupped her bottom and hoisted her against him. "What do you think?"

She gasped softly, and stared up at him in surprise. Richard watched her eyes grow dark with arousal. The cunning grin that slowly captured her features mesmerized him.

"I think we're wearing too many clothes," she replied huskily.

She slid her hands down to his chest and started unbuttoning his shirt. Her fingertips teased their way through the hair on his chest as she parted the shirtfront. She leaned forward and kissed his sternum. The pressure of her lips, still moist from their kiss, set him afire.

"In a hurry?" he asked, but the question came out more like a sigh than with the edge of droll irony he'd intended.

"I've been waiting seventeen years."

His arms tightened around her and he cradled her head against his chest with one hand. He kissed the top of her head. "You sure know how to put pressure on a man."

Barbara closed her eyes and listened to his heart beneath her ear. "You're not going to disappoint me."

"How can you be so sure?"

Like an old, familiar love song, the rhythmic beat of his heart stirred emotions and sparked memories of other times she had stood with her head nestled against his chest.

"Because it's already wonderful."

Her sigh fanned over his flesh, ruffling hairs and heating skin. "Barbara?" he asked.

"Mmm-hmm?"

"Which way is the bedroom?"

"In a hurry?" She teasingly threw his question back at him.

"I've been waiting seventeen years."

"You sure know how to put pressure on a woman."

He brushed her hair away from her temple and kissed her there. "You're not going to disappoint me."

"How can you be so sure?"

He kissed his way across her cheek, down to her mouth, and nibbled at her lips. "Because . . . it's . . . already—"

The kiss said it more eloquently than words. Words—passionate, fiery, tempestuous, intense, erotic, arousing—could only describe; the kiss *was*...all those things and more. By the time it ended in a duet of protesting groans, Richard's shirt was untucked and his hands were inside Barbara's sweater, roving over her smooth back. "You were right," he said. "We're wearing too many clothes."

"Your idea was good, too," she countered.

"Which idea?" he said. "You've inspired more than one."

"The bedroom," she said, taking his hand in hers. She led the way, but stopped abruptly in the doorway. The solemn expression on her face unsettled Richard.

"Cold feet?" he asked, terrified of her answer.

She looped her arms around his neck. "Nothing about me is cold right now."

"Then why the hesitation?"

"We finally crossed the threshold together." She smiled up at him cunningly. "I was just making sure I left my inhibitions at the door."

"What inhibitions?"

"Those nasty little gremlins that could try to stop me from enjoying every minute we're here together."

"Barbara, if you're not sure...if you have any doubts about this—"

"I left them at the door, remember?" Her voice grew very soft. "They were silly old doubts, anyway. I should have gotten rid of them seventeen years ago."

"You can't blame yourself for what happened?" He'd never even considered the idea that she might. "God, Barbara, you were . . . you have nothing to regret."

"If I hadn't been such a coward—"

"No, Barbara," he said, drawing her into his embrace. "God, no. You were the strong one. I was the one who messed up. I didn't have your strength."

"Strength isn't much company in bed."

Richard's heart swelled with tenderness. He'd known he'd hurt Barbara with his stupid betrayal, but he'd remembered her in an abstract way, as the innocent victim of his betrayal. He had imagined her brokenhearted and bitter, but his mind had turned her from a flesh-and-blood woman into a *symbol* of innocence. He'd never imagined her lying in bed, lonely and frustrated and blaming herself for what he'd screwed up.

He pulled her closer, needing the reassurance of her body next to his. "We've got so much to make up for." He kissed her forehead, her temple, her cheek. "So many lonely nights."

A sigh tore from Barbara's throat as she drew her head far enough away to see his face. "I agree. But I—this is so incredibly awkward. Richard, I need a few minutes in the bathroom. I'm not prepared—"

He peered into her eyes for a long moment. "Just don't change your mind."

"I'm not the one with a history of ambivalence," she said.

Richard's fingertips trembled as he lifted his hand to her face. He would have sacrificed anything within his power if he could have denied the accusation inherent in the comment or take away the pain that tinged it. "I'm not ambivalent anymore, Barbara. Just anxious."

She captured his hand and kissed his palm. "Me, too."

Music greeted her when she returned from the bathroom. Their special song floated in from the living room. Richard must have searched for it on the tape. The gesture, even more than the music, touched her heart.

Richard smiled endearingly and spread his arms in invitation, and she ran to him.

The old magic flared instantly between them. They hadn't taken four steps in time to the music before he was kissing her. At first, Barbara just let the magic mellow her, taking solace and comfort from the heat of arousal that curled through her while the familiar song swirled around them. Desire awakened inside her with its old persistence—strong, timeless, intoxicating.

It was the same as it always had been between them— only this time, they were adults. This time, they didn't have to stop.

Determinedly, she pushed Richard's shirt over his shoulders and down his arms, then feasted hungry hands on the smooth planes of his back. And when Richard, moaning into their kiss, hoisted her top up so his palms could roam at will over her back, she pushed away from him far enough to claw the sweater over her head and toss it aside.

Breathing heavily, Richard stared at her breasts, revealed but also concealed by delicate lace. "I'd forgotten. I remember every detail, but I'd also forgotten."

She knew exactly what he meant. She, too, remembered, but had forgotten. She remembered how wonderful it had been to feel Richard's chest under her cheek, how reassuring his arms were as he embraced her. But reality was so much better than a memory. She hadn't expected it to be better.

Reaching behind her, she unhooked her bra. Her breasts moved enticingly as she coaxed its slender straps down her arms.

Richard's gaze never wavered as he reached for her. He touched her cautiously, first grazing the valley between them with trembling fingertips, then the sides and then, gloriously, covering their swollen, sensitive tips with his palms.

"I'm as awed now as I ever was," he said, his voice a testament to the claim.

"And I'm as..." Sighing, she relaxed against him, letting her bare, heated flesh mold to his. His hand slid away as she allowed her breast to compress against his chest. Arms around his waist, she drew close and, clinging to him, implored, "Show me what I missed."

He went wild obliging her, touching, tasting. Each brush of his fingers, each stroke of his palms, each swipe of tongue or nip of teeth or unexpected little suckle was new and surprising and arousing. Barbara arched and clutched and strained against him; she tilted her head to allow his questing mouth access to her neck and moaned sensually while he discovered areas she'd never known were erogenous.

She tore at his slacks, he tore at hers until, finally, they were free of them. For a few suspended moments they stood looking at each other, touching only with their gazes. Heat flowed through Barbara's body like warm wax spilled from a candle. "No one's ever looked at me the way you do," she said. "As though—"

Her voice abandoned her as he splayed his hand over the top of her thigh. "Surely your husband—" he said, but she shook her head no.

"Dennis was not given to passion."

"Dennis was a fool."

"I don't want to talk about Dennis. I just want—" Gasping as his hand moved higher, she closed her eyes and threw back her head, savoring the pleasure of his caress. "I want you."

A hoarse sigh rushed from his throat as he lowered his mouth to hers for a plundering kiss. Hard muscle, body hair, heat, strength, restless hands, clever mouth—Barbara couldn't distinguish one from the other, couldn't divide them in her mind, didn't try. They were all part of Richard, making her feel things no other man had ever made her feel, making her want him, making her burn for fulfillment.

Locked in his embrace, she guided him to the bed and they toppled onto it together, then exchanged quizzical gazes and self-conscious giggles at the shock of finding themselves in bed together, nearly naked, with their arms and legs haphazardly tangled.

And then, suddenly, the momentary self-consciousness vanished, leaving only heated awareness between them.

Barbara's skin tingled with anticipation of the next brush, the next caress, the next taste. *So long*, she thought fiercely. She'd waited so long—

*Barbara*. Richard still couldn't believe that he was really here with her. The sweetness of having her next to him, naked except for a scrap of turquoise silk, begging him to take her with every ragged breath and sensual moan, was dizzying. If she wasn't so warm, if the scent of her hair wasn't so seductive, if her skin wasn't as alluring as satin under his fingertips, he might believe that he was dreaming, that he'd become so des-

perate to touch something fine and good that his mind
had conjured her out of his past.

But she was too warm, too solid, too human to be a
dream, and his desire for her was too human to be a
fantasy. He touched flesh and tasted woman. Her scent
filled his senses, her caressing hands drove him to frenzied need.

She rolled atop him, straddling him, and sighed lan-
guorously. Her eyes were hooded and dreamy, her lips
kiss-swollen. She gently guided his face to one side,
then kissed his neck just below his ear. "Does it feel as
good when I kiss you here as when I tickle you?"

"If it felt any better, I'd spontaneously combust."
Richard sounded as though he'd just run a marathon.

"I've never seen anyone spontaneously combust," she
said, then proceeded to torture him by fluttering the tip
of her tongue over the skin she'd just kissed.

"Let . . . me . . . show . . . you." He cupped her buttocks and pulled her closer.

She made a mewling sound of sheer physical yearning, then said breathlessly, "We're still wearing too
many clothes."

"Understatement of the century, Barbaloo." Never
had two scraps of fabric seemed more formidable than
the swatches of silk and cotton knit that separated
them. "Why don't we do something about it?"

"What did you have in mind?" Barbara asked, pushing up on hands and knees above him.

"Your breasts are incredible," he said, eyes transfixed.

Barbara lowered her bottom onto his thighs, and
mischievously slid her finger under the top elastic band

of his briefs and popped it. "You're not paying attention."

"Oh, yes. I am," he argued, still staring at her breasts.

"We were discussing our surplus of clothing," she said, taking hold of the elastic with both hands and heaving. With his cooperative tilt of hips, they gave way—everywhere except in the front. Barbara hooked her forefinger under the elastic to further lower the briefs, taking her sweet time as she did so. "Is that an Uzi in your pocket, or are you just glad to see me?"

"You're playing with fire," he warned.

Her gaze locked with his for a long moment. "It wouldn't be fair if just one of us was burning."

She finished pulling the briefs down, and eased them off.

Richard sat up, combed his fingers through her hair and cradled her head. "Your face," he said, imbuing the words with adoration and awe.

It seemed to Barbara that it took forever for his lips to reach hers, but she would willingly have waited forever for a kiss as sweet and slow and consuming. His mouth brushed hers, covered it, conquered it. His hands caressed and soothed as he coaxed her back down on the bed—into the fulfillment of a dream and the realization of half a lifetime of fantasies.

Every move seduced. Every touch excited. Every sound aroused. Barbara ceased to think, and simply responded, marveling in the miracle of being with Richard again—for the first time. She stroked, she sighed, she gasped under the magic of his loving touch. She held her breath as he peeled away the last of her clothing; trembled as he adored her with his eyes; cried out as his fingers caressed her in secret places.

"Barbara?"

Though his mouth was scarcely an inch from her ear, his voice seemed to come from far away. "Don't stop," she murmured.

His chuckle was a deep, sensual rumble. "Not a chance. But we need—"

She turned her head in his direction saying, "H-m-m? Oh. The trinket box on the table."

He found it easily and took out a foil packet. "You have me shaking like a schoolboy."

"Let me help." Her hand covered his, steadied it, drove him wild with needing her. And then she lay back and held her arms up in supplication. "Now," she said.

On the last whisper of a sigh, she added as he rolled astride her, "Finally."

Richard slid his hands up her arms to her hands and twined his fingers through hers, then kissed her with a sweetness and depth that made her squirm restlessly beneath him. He tore his mouth away from the kiss only long enough to utter a single word, a last concession to conscious thought before losing himself in their joining. "Finally."

Slowly he buried himself in her, moaning sensually as her soft, heated flesh molded around him. He let go of her hands to wrap his arms around her, desperate to hold her body as hard against him as possible.

Beneath him, Barbara moved restlessly, straining, clinging, pressing into him, clawing his back with open, loving hands that set his skin afire. Longer, wider, heavier than she, he seemed to surround her. His arms enfolded her. His legs locked with hers. It seemed almost as though he might absorb her, that they might just meld into a singular entity, and no prospect had ever seemed quite so sweet.

Frenzied, consumed by desire, desperate for relief from the unbearable pressure of longing building inside them, they struggled for the ancient rhythm that would bring them release. There were no mistakes, no errors in the quest; every motion tortured them with pleasure that brought them closer to fulfillment.

Though he fought for control, Richard reached the peak first, tensing in the throes of a climax that rocked him to his very soul. Barbara took the plunge scarce seconds behind him, hugging him with startling ferocity as though her very life depended upon having her arms around him.

Still joined, they lay together for an indeterminable period of time, waiting for their hearts to calm and their breathing to return to normal.

Barbara's first conscious awareness was of tender kisses on her temple and cheek. She felt the smile curve his lips as they settled on her neck and his sigh of repletion skittered hotly over her tingling skin.

She wanted to speak, to rejoice, but words eluded her, and would have been inadequate had she found them. She stroked his hair lovingly, terrified of the moment they would have to part, because she knew, deep in her heart, that when he rolled away from her, it would be like losing part of herself.

*All the years,* she thought. *All the wasted years.*

Eventually he eased away from her, gentle in his retreat, carefully shifting onto his side so he could cradle her as he nestled his face in the crook of her neck, with her hair next to his cheek.

The stereo clicked off. The resultant silence was rich and mellow and, somehow, appropriate to the moment. Barbara felt almost as though such a silence might freeze time so that they could remain exactly as they were forever, without having to think about mistakes of the past or uncertainties of the future.

Closing her eyes, she heaved a silent sigh and wished it could be so. She would have been perfectly content to spend forever here with Richard, with her shoulders wedged against his chest, and his arm around her. She lifted his hand to her mouth and kissed his palm, then pressed it between her breasts, above her heart.

"Told you so," Richard said.

"Hnmm?" She hadn't been expecting him to speak.

"I told you it wouldn't be simple between us."

Barbara rolled so that she could see his face. "Does that mean it was good for you?"

"No," he said, his expression stricken. "It wasn't *good* for me."

Goose pimples raised on Barbara's scalp. "It wasn't?"

"'Good for you' is one of those phrases strangers toss around after they've had lunch-hour sex, Barbara. It's a phrase people use to discuss sex without actually talking to each other."

He cradled her face and traced her lips with his thumb. "Somehow I just can't picture you in bed like this with a whole string of men asking, 'Was it good for you?' as though you were discussing the weather."

"I've never asked any man that before," she admitted.

"Then how could you ask me, of all people?" He drew in a pained breath. "God, Barbara, why would you even have to ask? You were here. You know how it was. It wasn't just good, any more than it was just sex."

She touched his face. "It was everything I ever dreamed it would be."

Richard closed his eyes, as if in pain, then forced them open again. "If it had been just sex, I'd be anxious to get out of this bed instead of wishing I never had to leave."

"Well," she sighed, "you said it wouldn't be simple."

His gaze locked with hers in silent communication. Barbara was almost afraid to speak, afraid of saying too much. She pulled his face down to hers.

Just before their lips met, she smiled seductively. "Didn't you also say it wouldn't be just once?"

# 7

"YOU DON'T MIND if we talk in the kitchen, do you?" Barbara said. "With the cooler weather, I've been in the mood for an old-fashioned pot roast, and if I don't put it on now, it won't be ready for dinner."

"No. That's okay," Missy said.

"Good," Barbara said, leading the way. Anticipating that Missy would be a bit ill-at-ease during her first visit, Barbara had wanted something active for them to do. Cooking, because it was so ordinary an activity, had seemed the most natural choice. "Would you like a glass of milk?"

"Okay."

"How about an apple?" Barbara asked, with her head in the refrigerator. "I'm going to have one."

"Thank you," Missy replied.

Barbara poured the milk, handed Missy the glass, and motioned for Missy to sit. She washed the apples and polished them, then took plates from the cabinet, knives from the drawer and a jar of peanut butter from the pantry and sat down across the table from Missy. "Would you like peanut butter on yours?"

"On an apple?" Missy asked skeptically, crinkling her nose—just as her father had the first time Barbara had offered him a peanut butter apple. Barbara's heart swelled with nostalgia as she recalled the distant afternoon when Richard had driven her home from school and she'd introduced him to the snack.

"My mom used to make me peanut butter apples when I was a little girl. Do you like peanut butter?"

"Sure."

"I'll make one, and you can try it. If you like it, I'll do the other one." She sliced one of the apples in two and cored each half, then filled the trenches with peanut butter.

Missy took one of the halves out of politeness and took a cautious nibble. "It's not too bad," she said, relieved.

Barbara, happy to note that the girl seemed to be relaxing, ate her half apple, then sliced the second apple and cored it. "With, or without?" she asked.

"With, I guess," Missy said, smiling shyly.

Barbara returned her smile, prepared the apple, then rose. "I'd better get that roast on."

She took the meat and vegetables from the refrigerator, then put the meat on a cutting board and sliced away the narrow edge of fat. Sensing Missy's attention on her as she worked, Barbara said, "I always like pot roast when the weather gets like this."

Missy didn't comment. Barbara took several containers from the spice cabinet and lined them up on the counter. Then she picked up the pepper grinder, ground a generous portion over the roast and rubbed it in with her fingertips. Missy was still watching her interestedly, and Barbara decided it was time for a gamble.

"Can you give me a hand here?" she asked, and then, seeing the look of helplessness on Missy's face, quickly continued, "I always rub before I finish sprinkling, then

I end up having to wash my hands two or three times. If you'd just sprinkle while I rub—"

"Okay," Missy said, dubious but willing.

"Paprika first," Barbara said.

Missy hesitated, so Barbara added encouragingly, "Just take the lid off the bottle. It's a shaker top. You just sprinkle it on."

Missy did as she said, and gave the bottle a tenuous shake.

Barbara rubbed in the spice and turned the meat over. "This side. And don't worry. Paprika is pretty mild. You can't have too much."

Missy was more confident this time.

"Now the ground cloves," Barbara said. As Missy sprinkled, she added, "Smells good, doesn't it?"

Missy nodded, and Barbara grinned conspiratorially. "It's my secret pot roast ingredient."

"You must like to cook," Missy said.

"Since I live alone, it would be easy to fast food it all the time, but I try to cook real meals at least a couple of times a week. Let's see...now, the garlic powder, and then we're ready for the flour."

Missy opened the garlic powder and sprinkled. "I thought flour was for bread and cake and stuff."

"You don't use much. Just enough to coat the meat. It's called dredging. It makes the meat brown prettier and thickens the stock while the meat's cooking."

"You're a good cook, huh?"

Barbara laughed softly. "My grandmother was a good cook. She taught me."

"My grandma's a neatness freak. She never lets me in the kitchen because she's afraid I'll make a mess."

Deliberately downplaying the information, Barbara shrugged. "Well, now you have *my* secret pot roast ingredient—in case you want to try making pot roast sometime."

"You think I could?"

Barbara shrugged. "Why not? By the time we finish in a few minutes, you'll be an old pro. The flour's in that plastic canister. There's a sifter inside. Just sift a little bit over each side while I rub it in. That's good. See? It doesn't take much."

"It looks funny."

Barbara scrutinized the spiced and floured hunk of beef. "It does look a bit . . . disreputable. But trust me, it'll be delicious." She stepped to the sink to wash her hands. "Want to help with the vegetables?"

"Okay."

"There's a clean cutting board and a fresh knife in that drawer," Barbara said, breaking two stalks from the bunch of celery. "You can slice these as soon as I get them washed."

Missy hesitated, chewing on her bottom lip before saying, "I'm not very good at slicing."

"Well," said Barbara, "get the board and the knife and we'll work on that. What seems to be the problem?"

"I can't make them . . . you know, the same size."

Barbara leaned over and whispered in Missy's ear. "For pot roast, it doesn't matter!"

Missy pulled a doubtful face.

"It's true!" Barbara said. "For a side dish, the pieces need to be the same size so they can cook uniformly. But with pot roast, the vegetables are just for flavoring, and to keep the meat moist. So it's a great way to practice. And practice is all it really takes."

They progressed from celery to carrots, with Barbara showing Missy how to cut off the tops and tips, to an onion, over which they both shed tears, laughing over the absurdity of crying. After demonstrating how to brown the dredged meat on all edges before adding the vegetables and water and reducing the heat, Barbara announced, "And now, we can kick back and relax."

"How long will it take to cook?" Missy asked on the way to the living room.

"That depends on the weight of the meat and how you like it cooked," Barbara said. "I like pot roast falling apart tender, so it'll probably take two to three hours."

In the living room, Missy moved as if to sit down, then hesitated self-consciously.

"Just make yourself at home," Barbara said. "You can kick off your shoes and lie down on the couch if you'd like."

"Like at a shrink's?" Missy asked cautiously.

It was so unexpected, so off-the-wall and yet so logical at the same time, that Barbara chuckled. "I'm not a psychiatrist, Missy. I just thought that you might want to relax after a long day at school. You can sit in the armchair and prop your feet on the coffee table if you'd rather."

"Can I unsnap my jeans? They're kind of tight."

"Sure you can. There's nobody here but us girls." She tried to sound nonchalant. "You're going to have to get some maternity clothes soon."

"I guess so."

"Don't you like to shop?"

Missy made a face. "Heather and I go to the mall sometimes, but—"

"Earrings are more interesting than maternity pants?"

Missy nodded sullenly.

"What about your dad? Do you shop with him?"

"Not very often. He doesn't know much about...you know, clothes."

"Maybe you and I could go some afternoon. I love to shop."

Missy seemed to want to speak, but didn't, so Barbara took a different tack. "Would you like some music? I have a new tape of songs that were popular when I was your age."

"Okay."

Barbara turned on the stereo, then settled in the armchair opposite the coffee table from Missy. "Your dad would probably remember some of these," Barbara said, careful not to make the observation seem too important. "We went to the same high school. Did he tell you?"

Missy nodded.

"It was quite a surprise seeing a face from the past."

After a thoughtful silence, Missy asked tremulously, "Did you know my mother, too?"

It was the most logical question in the world, but Barbara was blindsided by it. She hesitated, composing her reply before answering. "Not very well. She was a couple of years older than I was, so we didn't have classes together or anything."

"Do I look like her?"

The expression in the girl's eyes as Barbara studied Missy's expectant face tore Barbara apart inside. She tried earnestly to remember Christine's face and make a mental comparison, but the only image of the young woman that came to mind was the one of her wearing a smug, self-satisfied smirk as she had hung on Richard's arm at the football game. All Barbara saw when she looked at Missy was a troubled child-woman. And all she could think of was that this was Richard's daughter who was in so much trouble. "I think you favor your father more, but that could be because it's been so long since I saw Christine."

Missy looked away. "Grandmother thinks I'm just like her."

"You probably are a little bit like your mother, Missy. You're also a little like your father, and a little like your grandmother, and a little like every person who's been important to you. The special blend you are makes you a unique person. It'll be the same with your baby."

Missy had grown thoughtfully quiet. Barbara waited a while before initiating conversation again. "Earlier I told you that I'm not a psychiatrist, and that's true. I just want to be your friend, in case you need one. But I want you to know that you can trust me, Missy. If you need to talk—about anything—you can talk to me, and anything you tell me will stay between the two of us."

"You won't tell . . . *anybody?*"

"Not if you didn't want me to."

"Not even my daddy?"

*Not even her daddy!* The realization hit Barbara then of what a precarious and potentially compromising position she was in, counseling Missy while sleeping

with Richard. It was not nearly so simple as it had
seemed when she and Richard had agreed, in the afterglow of lovemaking, that they should keep their relationship confidential for a while. Richard had explained
that he felt Missy's life was in enough turmoil with her
pregnancy; he did not wish to add to her emotional load
by asking her to adjust to his rather sudden, but quite
serious, romantic involvement with a woman.

"If there was something I thought he needed to know,
then I would encourage you to talk to him, but no, I
wouldn't violate a confidence."

She waited for Missy to respond. As usual, Missy
surprised her. "Could we really go shopping?"

"We'd have to get your dad's permission, but I'd love
it. We could go next week. Instead of coming here."

"Okay." Missy hesitated, as though deciding whether
to commit herself further, then said, "I really need some
stuff bad. I need . . . bras."

"I'm not surprised," Barbara replied. "Your breasts
change a lot when you're pregnant. Did you know that?
I mean, that it's normal for your breasts to change?"

"Yeah. It's in a book the doctor gave me. I just—" she
shrugged "I didn't want to ask for . . . you know."

"Maternity bras?"

Missy nodded.

"Well, maybe it won't be so bad if we ask for them
together." She smiled reassuringly. "That's the kind of
thing I was hoping I could help you with. Girl stuff. If
you have any concerns about your pregnancy, physical or otherwise, we can talk about those."

Though quiet, Missy appeared receptive, so Barbara decided to take a big chance. "We could talk about

how you feel about the baby, or about the baby's father."

She had touched a chord. Missy paled, and sadness clouded her eyes. "I don't see him anymore." Embarrassed, she turned her gaze away from Barbara's as she confessed, "He goes to another school, but that's not the only reason I don't see him. His mother won't let him see me. She thinks that I . . . that it's my fault."

*His mother won't let him!* It was ludicrous enough to make her groan and sad enough to break her heart. Two young people expecting a child, and the father's mother wouldn't let them see each other. She was left little time to think about it, though, because suddenly Missy released a heart-rending sob.

"It's not true, Ms. Wilson. Everything she said. It wasn't true. I didn't get pregnant on purpose. We were using a condom, but it busted. I didn't plan the whole thing."

Barbara grabbed a box of tissue and took them to Missy, perching on the arm of Missy's chair so she could put her arm around her to comfort her. "People often say things when they're upset that they know aren't true. I'm sure this boy's mother didn't believe everything she said."

"She did," Missy said, curving into Barbara's embrace. "She did. Oh, Ms. Wilson, she called me a slut, and Josh just sat there, and then my dad asked him how he could just sit there and not say anything when he knew good and well that I was a virgin when I met him, and Josh's mother said she doubted that. Then Josh tried to tell her and she told him to shut up because he was too naive to know what I was up to, and that she wasn't even convinced the baby was Josh's."

She sniffed mightily. "It was so awful."

Barbara hugged and rocked her. "Of course it was. It must have been horrible for you."

The story poured from Missy, as if she'd been holding it in, just waiting for the right moment to tell someone. "She said that if I was going to sleep around, that I should have been responsible enough to make sure I didn't get pregnant, and that girls can do a lot more about it than guys. And then she said that Josh was too young to be a father, and that I wouldn't be a good mother, and that if I had any sense, I'd have an abortion, and I said no, that I didn't want to kill my baby."

She drew away to blow her nose. Barbara went to the bathroom for a damp cloth, then sat down on the floor in front of Missy's chair and patted Missy on the knee. "How did Josh's mother react when you told her you wanted to keep the baby?"

Missy bathed her face with the damp cloth, then swallowed. "She called me a bunch of names again, and Daddy told her to shut up and said that she couldn't talk to me that way, and that Josh was just as responsible as I was. And Josh's mother said that if I didn't have an abortion that I would be ruining Josh's life and my life and the baby's, and that it wasn't fair that Josh should have to pay for my stupidity. And she said that if we expected Josh to support the baby, that we'd have to get a blood test after the baby was born to prove that Josh was really the father."

She sobbed, and pressed the cloth to her face. Her voice was thin as she continued. "Daddy was really,

really mad, and he said that if Josh didn't want to live up to his responsibility, he would have to agree to give up any right to the baby, ever, and Josh's mother said that was just fine, just to send the papers over and Josh would be more than happy to sign them. And Josh . . . Josh just sat there. He didn't say a thing."

"That must have hurt you very badly."

Missy buried her face in the washcloth. "I thought—"

"You thought he cared more about you."

Missy nodded frantically.

"And you must have cared a great deal about him, or you wouldn't have made love with him."

Missy froze, then turned slowly to face Barbara. She sniffed pitifully, then released a sigh of such relief that Barbara wondered that a person's lungs could have held so much air. "He's the only one, ever."

Then with eyes so pleading that Barbara thought her heart surely would break for the girl, Missy asked, "You believe me, don't you?"

Moving back to the arm of the chair, Barbara embraced Missy and hugged her tightly—as tightly as she would have held any child of her own who was aching. "Oh, Missy, yes, I believe you. Of course I believe you. Your father does, too. And he loves you very much. And your grandmother—"

She knew instantly she'd made a mistake as Missy turned to stone and said vehemently, "I wish I didn't have to tell my grandmother, ever. She thinks—"

The thought trailed into a shuddering sigh. Barbara would have given a month of lunches to know what Missy was so convinced her grandmother would think about her pregnancy, but after a prolonged pause, Missy lifted her head and, chin quivering, repeated, simply, "I wish she never had to know."

Barbara smoothed a strand of hair from Missy's moist cheek. "When do you plan to tell her?"

"Daddy says we can wait until she gets back from her trip in April."

"That gives you time to think about the best way to approach her." She gave Missy a gentle hug. "You know, once she's past the initial shock, she may surprise you by being very understanding. After all, the baby inside you is her great-grandchild."

Missy's sniff somehow managed to convey skepticism, but she was much calmer. Pleased with the way Missy had opened up to her, Barbara remained silent, letting Missy decide which direction their discussion would take.

She didn't take it in an easy direction. She posed the question softly, so softly that Barbara wouldn't have been able to hear it if she hadn't been so close to her. "Do you think I should have had an abortion, like Josh's mother said?"

It was the last question in the world Barbara wanted to hear. "I'm probably not the right person to answer that question, Missy, because I can't be objective. But I can tell you this—I think you did what your heart told you to do, and sometimes that's the only thing a woman can do when she's trying to make that decision."

Missy contemplated Barbara's reply for a while, then asked, "Why did you say that you couldn't be objective?"

*Who's counseling whom?* Barbara thought, trying to decide how much of herself to share. But, since she had nothing to hide and she was trying to win Missy's confidence, she answered the question frankly. "Because I've always wanted a child, and that makes it impossible for me to think of abortion as a solution without thinking about the babies I've never had. When I see a nice young woman like you, with her life ahead of her, I think, up here—" she pointed to her temple "—about how an unplanned baby would complicate her life, economically and socially and educationally. So I can understand why abortion would be an appealing option. I know women are desperate sometimes. But, in here—" she patted her heart "—in here, I can't help thinking about the babies and thinking that, sometimes, life is unfair, both to the women who want babies and can't have them, and to the ones who are pregnant and don't want to be."

"Why don't you adopt a baby?"

"I might have, if my husband and I hadn't divorced. But we did, and I put my energy into other things. I finished my master's degree, then became a guidance counselor."

"Single women have babies."

"Yes. But parenting is hard work, and if I had a child, I would want to be sure I could give it all the nurturing it needed, and that would be difficult with the job I have. My students help fill the empty place where my child would be. It's almost as if I get a couple of hundred kids every year."

Missy exhaled a soft sigh. "My doctor says that she has patients who can't have children, and that if I want to give my baby up for adoption, that she could help find a good home for it."

"Are you considering adoption for your baby?" Barbara didn't know why the prospect had not occurred to her before.

Missy shrugged. "The lawyer who drew up the papers for Josh to sign said that if I wanted to put the baby up for adoption, Josh can't stop me."

"How do you feel about that?"

Missy grew very still. "It would be a lot easier than trying to raise a baby. And it might be better for the baby." Her chin succumbed to one little quiver before she was able to reclaim her composure. "But I'd never get to see my baby again. I think I'd be sad."

*Sad*, Barbara thought morosely. God, it was the epitome of understatement. How many women had she heard describe the life-long anguish of giving up a child? Reunification stories of long separated parents and children who'd been searching for each other had almost become cliché on television talk shows.

But if "sad" was an understatement when used to describe the angst of giving up a child, so was the term "not easy" when used to describe the difficulties that raising a child would present to a young woman like Missy. Motherhood would forever change her life, cutting short her early youth by throwing her into one of the most adult roles in society.

There was no simple solution, no quick fix, no painless alternative to Missy's situation. Or Richard's, in his role as Missy's father. Missy felt guilty. Richard felt responsible. Both were tormented.

Barbara realized suddenly that she had rushed headlong into their torment with her heart totally exposed. And that the only thing any of them could be sure of was that from this point on, all of their lives would be irrevocably changed.

# 8

BARBARA HAD JUST stepped out of the shower when the phone rang. She answered with a standard hello.

"If I don't kiss you within the next hour, I may explode" came the reply.

"Richard!" The name rushed forth as her heart danced at the sound of his voice.

"I, uh, could sneak away from home for a while if I thought a certain woman would welcome my company."

"I just finished showering," she said. "Should I dress?"

"Not on my account."

But she did dress—in a floor-length gown of red, lace-trimmed chiffon, an extravagant garment that she'd bought on a whim and kept wrapped in tissue, saving it for a special night.

Like tonight.

And a special man.

Like Richard.

He arrived within the hour with a bottle of wine and a supermarket bouquet of flowers, but the wine went unopened, and the flowers never made it into a vase.

He had not planned to take her with the ardor and haste of a soldier returning home from the Crusades after a decade of abstinence, but he hadn't anticipated that she'd be wearing a garment as wispy as thin fog, or that she would greet him with a smile as warm as sunshine and a kiss as hot as the sun itself. He hadn't expected her to reach out to him with hands that were, at once, greedy and generous, taking and giving pleasure as she eagerly loosened his clothing and stroked his body.

It was the first time a woman had ever undressed him that way, as though she could hardly wait to touch him. Her breath fanned hotly over his skin as she planted short, moist kisses along his shoulder blade, and then on his chest, to his sternum. She moved lower, zigzagging across his ribs and midriff until she reached the waistband of his slacks, which she unhooked and unzipped with an endearing and arousing blend of impatience and inexperience. She peeled them off, chasing them down his thighs with tiny kisses, coaxing one foot, then the other up so she could remove his shoes and pull his pants over them.

When she pressed her lips to his thigh again, the intensity was unbearable. Richard knelt, bringing his face level with hers. He set the wine aside on the floor and handed Barbara the bouquet. She lifted it to smell a rose that was just beginning to open. There was something in the gesture that cast them into roles as old as time: the fair maiden and the lovestruck beau.

Never had Richard been more aware of his own manhood as when he looked at Barbara's face framed by those flowers. Soft, sensual, gentle, she evoked in him a feeling of strength and power too elemental to fall subject to political correctness. In that instant he wanted her so badly that he would have died to possess her, and he loved her so thoroughly that he would have killed to protect her.

His gaze never parted with hers as he covered the smile forming on her mouth with a deep, claiming kiss. Wrapping one arm around his neck, she lay back on the floor, pulling him with her, and the flowers went the way of the forgotten wine bottle as his body settled over hers.

The gown, so seductive and feminine, turned out, like a woman, to possess strength that defied its delicate appearance. The springy, crawly chiffon took on a life of its own as it fought Richard's every effort to touch Barbara skin to skin, binding and bunching in opposition to his every move. Thin, sheer, frail-looking, the fabric nevertheless separated them as efficiently as a suit of mail.

Finally, with a groan of frustration, Richard rolled aside and sat up.

"What is it?" Barbara asked with effort.

Staring, Richard took in her bruised lips, her flushed face, her breasts rising and falling with labored breathing. He'd never seen a woman more ready for loving. "It's war," he growled. "Plain and simple. I have met the enemy, and it is a formidable foe."

Barbara was trying to concentrate. "War? Enemy?"

Richard gathered a handful of chiffon and crushed it in his fist. "It's this or me, Barbaloo. Make your choice."

Grinning, Barbara teased, "I should choose the gown on the grounds that you called me . . . that name." He'd first taunted her with the name after she'd confided that her middle name was Louise.

"But—" she leaned toward him and slid her hand across his chest "—since you called me that the first night we made love, it has sort of acquired sentimental connotations, so . . ."

Her hand moved lower. Her fingers tantalized. With a look that told her she was playing with fire, he stood abruptly, then extended his hand to help her up. "Come on. As long as we have to stop what we were doing to get rid of that gown, we might as well find someplace more comfortable."

"Good idea," Barbara agreed. "That floor is almost as hard as you are."

"Forged steel is not as hard as I am right now," he said drolly.

Barbara smiled coquettishly. "Why don't you quit bragging and make love to me . . . *Ricky?*"

She was off before the hated nickname had fully parted her tongue, and he was right behind her, following her into the bedroom, where she stopped next to the bed.

"Even my mother knows better than to call me Ricky!" he said, feeling greatly at a disadvantage in his socks and undershorts, while she looked so regal in that dratted gown with the full circular skirt billowing around her.

Barbara yanked the bedspread and top sheet back and plumped the nearest pillow. Then she perched on the edge of the bed, her brilliant gown draped widely, and smiled cunningly. "Why don't you show me why I shouldn't?"

Dare him, would she? Richard yanked off one sock, then the other, then his briefs, then stalked to the bed, stopping within feet of her. "Exhibit A."

Barbara's eyes narrowed and her expression softened. She drew in a soft, deep breath and then reached out with trembling fingers to stroke him. "Very impressive," she said with wonder in her voice.

The intimate caress rushed through Richard with the force of a physical blow. Staggered by the intensity of it, he dropped onto the bed beside her. She urged him backward, until he was lying down, and wrapped her hand around him.

"Hard as forged steel," she cooed.

The sound of her voice, hoarse with passion, and the sight of her touching him was almost as arousing as the actual pressure of her fingers. He watched as she opened a packet from the trinket box and sheathed him. He felt slightly detached, as if viewing a scene through a telescope, yet, at the same time, he was fully cognizant of the pressure of her fingers as she unrolled the condom, of the color rising in her cheeks as she explored in minute detail the shape and size of him, of the change in her breathing as she became increasingly aroused.

Gathering the wide skirt of her gown and draping it over his chest, she moved astride him, emitting a guttural sigh as she took him inside her. With his arms and hands beneath the gown, he was able, finally, to touch her the way he longed to. He explored the curve of her waist, stroked the small of her back, kneaded the fullness of her hips, filling his hands with her as she undulated above him.

Her lovemaking consumed his every thought and every sensation until, finally, she tensed and cried his name and her body convulsed around him. He climaxed soon afterward, glorying in the miracle of the pleasure that he brought to her. She was there, in his arms, stroking his hair, kissing his cheeks gently, pulling the million fragments of him back together.

Eventually, Barbara eased off him and lay beside him. Richard turned onto his side, draping an arm and leg over her to hold her near. For several minutes they remained there, nestled together, silent except for the sound of their breathing, before Richard kissed Barbara on the cheek and told her he'd be right back.

He rejoined her quickly and draped his arm across her pillow, inviting her to snuggle. She did so enthusiastically and said, "Welcome back. I missed you."

"I hurried."

"I missed you, anyway."

Nuzzling her hair aside, he kissed her nape. "I missed you, too. That's why I hurried. God, you smell good."

"You caught me right out of the shower."

A minute, perhaps two, passed before he said, "Barbara?"

"Oo-oo-oo," she groaned. "I hope it's not too serious."

"What?"

"The question that's imminent after you say my name that way. I hope it's not too . . . difficult." She rolled so she could see his face, at least in profile. "This moment is too nice to mess up with anything tough."

"It's not tough. I'm just . . . curious about something."

"Fire away, then."

"In the bathroom—I couldn't help noticing the birth control package."

"The sponge."

"Mmm-hmm. And I just wondered . . . I thought—"

Barbara sighed dismally. "That I was sterile?"

Richard nodded.

"I'm not sterile."

"But you said—"

"I said I couldn't have children. *Dennis* and I couldn't have children."

"*Dennis* was sterile?"

"Not completely. His sperm were a little sluggish, but that wasn't the reason he and I couldn't make a baby. Our . . . I guess you'd call it 'individual body chemistries' were incompatible. The doctors said it wasn't entirely impossible, but it would be close to miraculous if it happened."

"There was nothing they could do about it?"

"Nothing that Dennis would have tolerated," she replied, then smiled softly at his look of consternation. "Dennis found the various tests for fertility embarrassing. Any other humiliating procedures were out of the question."

The sadness in her eyes tore at Richard's heart. It was the same sadness that always haunted her eyes when she talked about her marriage. Lifting his hand to her face, he traced her lips with his thumb. "I didn't mean to dredge up painful memories."

"They're not painful," she said. "Just . . . sad. It would have been much simpler if I had been infertile. That way, Dennis could have blamed me outright."

"He would have blamed you?"

"Dennis was a tidy man. He liked to assign blame. When he couldn't, it offended his sense of order. So when he decided that it was time to have a child, and I didn't get pregnant, I was tested. And tested. And tested. And when the tests came up with no answers, the doctors suggested that Dennis—"

She shook her head. "I think I knew our marriage was over the day Dennis threw a fit because he had to deposit sperm in a cup." Her attitude changed to one of defiance as she remembered. "I'd been poked and prodded and stuck with needles and probed with cameras, and he found it humiliating to deposit sperm in a cup. He was *offended* by the dirty magazines they kept in the rooms for the convenience of the patients. After that, we were just going through the motions."

Richard rolled atop her and cradled her face in his hands. "I should have found you a long time ago. I should have looked for you. I tried to do the right thing with Christine, but when it was obvious it would never work, I should have turned heaven and earth over to find you."

The intensity in his eyes was frightening. Barbara couldn't believe what he was suggesting. "Richard, what are you saying? I was married. I was committed to making my marriage work. Do you think I would have just walked away because I got a better offer?"

"Of course not." He exhaled a sigh of pure anguish and closed his eyes for a moment, as if shutting away pain, then opened them again to look at her face. "I don't know what to think anymore. I just know that nothing has ever felt as right as having you next to me like this, and that if it had taken a hundred years instead of seventeen, I would have felt the same way when I walked into your office and saw you. And I know that no matter how badly I've managed to screw up my life, and no matter how confused I am about everything else that is going on, that this . . . *this*—"

He kissed her ruggedly, not gently but with a wealth of feeling, and when he tore his mouth from hers, he was breathing heavily. As was Barbara. "Us," he continued. "You. Me. Here. Together like this—this is right."

"I can't argue with you," she said, driving her fingers into his hair. "I'd be lying if I tried."

She pulled his head down, lifting hers from the pillow to meet him. The kiss was immediately deep and desperate, and so was the lovemaking that followed.

"Are you okay? I didn't hurt you, did I?" Richard asked when his power of speech returned.

"Hurt me?" Barbara asked, still gloriously, gloriously fulfilled. Her gown was in a cloudlike heap on the far side of the room, and the bedding looked as though it had been whipped by a tornado.

Barbara herself felt as if she wore the mark of his possession from head to feet, wore it in the form of whisker burns, kiss-bruised lips, hopelessly disheveled hair, and flushed, tingling skin. "Don't you know," she said somewhat breathlessly, "that some women wait an entire lifetime to have the kind of sex we just had? I feel as though I've had every single inch of you."

"You'd have to turn me inside out to find an inch of me you didn't," he said.

Barbara stretched languidly. "There's a lot to be said for seventeen years' worth of fantasy for foreplay."

"There's even more to be said for being with the right person," Richard said.

Barbara's grin was positively lewd as she admitted, "There is a certain amount of chemistry between us."

"Something along the lines of nitro and glycerine," Richard said. "Which makes it doubly frustrating to think about all the years we've wasted."

"Spilt milk," Barbara said. "Let's just . . . enjoy the here and now and try not to devote too much energy on regrets. Things have a way of working out in their own good time."

"I can't touch you without thinking about all the times I should have been touching you and wasn't."

"Sexually speaking, this is the very best time I could have linked up with you."

Richard looked at her askance.

"It's true," she said. "If we'd made love when you were nineteen, you would have been at your sexual peak. Now I'm at mine. So, technically, it would have been better for you back then, but it's better for me now."

Richard chortled. "If it had been any better, I'd be in the emergency room."

"See?" she teased. "You would never have said that at nineteen. You'd be looking around for more."

"If you're trying to tell me you'd like a little more, I'm a dead man. You may make me feel nineteen again, but my working parts are definitely thirty-something."

Barbara laughed. "With men, it's an endurance thing. With women, it's more a contented glow type of thing."

He gathered her into his arms for a loud, playful kiss. "I can't tell you how relieved I am to hear that."

"I could use a shower," Barbara said, pushing up on one elbow.

"I thought you just got out of the shower."

"You've undone all that," she said.

"I could be persuaded to scrub your back," Richard said. "As long as you promise not to take advantage of me when we're all slippery."

"My working parts are thirty-something, too," she assured him.

"Well, then—"

They were not even off the bed when the phone rang. "It's after ten," Barbara said, alarmed.

"It's probably Missy," Richard said sheepishly. "I came here from my office and had the calls on my back line forwarded."

"Then you answer," Barbara said. "She might recognize my voice."

Richard nodded. "I'm sorry. I honestly didn't think about how compromising it would be for you to have a man answering your phone this time of night."

The phone rang a second time. "For Pete's sake, answer it," Barbara said. "If someone asks for me, tell them they have the wrong number. They'll think they misdialed and call back."

Richard picked up the phone on the bedside table. "R. Blake." He gave Barbara a thumbs-up sign as he continued. "Hi, sweetheart. Did you find what you needed at the library?" He listened for a moment. "You're not feeling bad, are you? Oh. Good. Okay. You do that. I shouldn't be too much longer. Another hour or so. You lock up good and tight. Yeah. I'm glad you called. Good night."

He hung up the phone and looked at Barbara. "We're, uh, still getting used to our independence since my mother left. If I have to be away after dark, I like to check in with her, or vice versa. She met a study group at the library tonight. They're working on some project."

"You don't have to explain parenthood to me," Barbara said. "I wish more of my students had parents like you. You'd be surprised how many parents really don't know where their kids are most of the time."

"Excuse me," he said with a grin, "but I'm having a bit of a problem thinking of you as a guidance counselor when you're standing in front of me naked as the day you were born."

"And I'm having a bit of a problem thinking of you as a conscientious parent when you're having to sneak around to see me and having calls forwarded from your office."

"I won't do that anymore if you don't want me to. I should have checked with you first."

"It's not the phone. I don't mind that. Missy has to be able to get in touch with you. It's . . . I feel like I'm involved with a married man."

"It won't be like this forever."

She smiled drolly. "Isn't that what married men always tell their mistresses?"

"Mmm-hmm," he said sensuously. "Just before they scrub their backs."

"Your turn," she said later, after he'd scrubbed her back and a lot of equally important regions. "Hand me that bar of soap."

"Soap? I like this slippery stuff better."

"You can't go home smelling like an English garden!"

"As if I don't already," he said, hugging her a little tighter.

She turned in his arms to face him and took a step back. "We'll just have to scrub all that sissy, girlie stuff off you, won't we?"

She wet the soap and slid it in circles over his chest and ribs. "See? Soap isn't so bad."

"I'll never think of soap the same way again," he said, closing his eyes as she reached her arms around his waist to lather his back.

She was still, he noted with much satisfaction, quite slippery in all the best places.

Later, they patted each other dry. Richard walked through the apartment collecting his clothes and donning garments one by one. When he was finally dressed, he found Barbara stretched out on the sofa in a terry wrap robe. She had lit several votive candles on the coffee table.

He stood for a moment, absorbing the sight of her. "You don't look a day older than you did seventeen years ago."

Pulling herself up into a sitting position, Barbara smiled and patted the sofa cushion. "Join me."

He sat where she indicated. "Don't get too comfortable," he warned as she snuggled up to him.

"Too late," she murmured, leaning her back against his chest. "I'm already comfortable."

"I really can't stay."

"I know," she said. "But for a few minutes we can pretend."

"Like we used to."

"Mmm-hmm."

"Talk about déjà vu. Who would have thought that I'd still be kissing you good-night and then having to sneak home when I'm thirty-six years old?"

"It won't be this way forever."

"We used to say that, too," Richard said grimly.

Barbara sighed. "We haven't even talked."

"I liked what we did better than talking."

"We need to talk about Missy."

"I hear you two are going shopping."

"She's supposed to ask you if it's all right. You don't mind, do you? She needs some . . . female things and some maternity clothes."

"I've already given her my credit card. I'll be eternally grateful to you for taking her. My mother always handled the shopping. I wouldn't be much help to Missy even if I went with her."

"I thought I'd take her to one of the Orlando malls. If we went out here in the 'burbs and she ran into some of her friends, she might be embarrassed to be caught with a teacher. She's already self-conscious enough about needing maternity clothes."

"I'm glad you two are—what's the latest word?— bonding? She's been a little . . . I don't know how to describe it. Preoccupied and . . . quiet."

Concern weighted Barbara's voice, as it had Richard's. "She desperately needs a confidante—a female confidante—and I'm glad to be there for her. But I still have some mixed feelings about this situation, Richard. For Missy's sake, I hope I'm not in over my head. "

"She likes you," Richard said. "That's just as important as any diploma you could have. If we tried to hoist her off on a stranger, I think she'd clam up."

"You know her better than I do," Barbara said. "I just hope your instincts are on target." She paused pensively, then asked, "Did you know she was considering giving her baby up for adoption?"

"The subject came up with the lawyer who drew up the release papers for the father to sign."

"How do you feel about that?"

"That sounds like a counselor-type question," Richard said, and Barbara felt him tense.

"It's an occupational hazard," she said apologetically. "You don't have to answer."

Richard released a dismal sigh. "I'm sorry, Barbara. I know you're concerned. It's just . . . I don't know how to answer. How in the hell am I supposed to feel about it? I haven't even assimilated the idea of Missy's being pregnant, much less come to terms with what she's going to do with a baby. I think about her saddled with a child and it seems so . . . unfair. God, she's still a baby herself."

"She's not a baby, Richard."

"Obviously." The word held bitterness and frustration. "But no matter how old or how grown up she gets, to me she'll always be that little baby girl I held in my hands." His eyes met hers gravely. "She was that tiny. I could literally hold her in my hands."

His arms crossed over Barbara's midsection. Barbara guided his hands to her mouth and kissed them, backs first, then palms. Then she pressed them to her face. "These are good hands for anyone to be in."

Richard smiled sadly at her attempt to cheer him. "I was more terrified of that tiny little bundle than I'd ever been of anything in my entire life. And I'm just as terrified now, for her."

"She has a difficult decision to make."

"Difficult?" He shook his head. "Try impossible. I know my daughter. When she cares, she cares with her whole heart. As inconceivable as it is to picture her trying to raise a child at this point in her life, I can't imagine her handing someone a baby she's given birth to, knowing she'd never see it again. No matter what she does, some part of her is going to be destroyed."

He shook his head and chortled bitterly. "The kid has one boyfriend and her life is topsy-turvy. It's history repeating itself."

"You've got to quit equating your experience with Missy's situation. They're not the same."

"No," he said forlornly. "I guess they're not. We both slept with the wrong person for the wrong reason, but I did it because I was young and didn't have the good sense to know how to handle hormones. Missy—" His voice choked with emotion. "Missy just had a bad example when she was vulnerable."

"Do you honestly think Missy wouldn't have gone to bed with her boyfriend if she hadn't surprised you in your little indiscretion?"

"Yes. I'm sure of it."

"You don't think peer pressure and today's sex-saturated media had anything to do with it? Richard, teenage girls feel *everything* strongly. She probably thought she was truly in love with this boy."

"With that spineless little wimp?"

"Spoken like a true father," Barbara said.

Richard sniffed indignantly. "I'd be doing society a favor if I castrated that little jerk. He didn't think twice about taking an innocent girl to bed, but when he got found out, he didn't even have the balls to stand beside her and own up to what he'd done."

"How old is he?"

"Sixteen."

"Just a kid," Barbara said. "He's probably scared to death."

"So's Missy."

Barbara didn't have an answer for that. In the silence that ensued, she became aware of Richard again, warm and firm next to her. She rested her head against his chest and listened to his heart, then urged his hand to her lips and kissed the tops of his fingers.

"You're not making it any easier for me to leave."

"There are things I'd like to make easier for you," she said. "Leaving me isn't one of them."

"It won't be this way forever," he said.

This time he sealed the promise with a kiss.

# 9

THE TRAFFIC was four lanes wide in each direction. The signal light had already gone through its cycle twice while Barbara and Missy waited their turn in the left hand turn lane. "Is the traffic always like this?" Missy asked.

"It's worse on weekends and holidays," Barbara said. "But it's worth it. I try to get over here a couple of times a year."

"Heather's big sister got her prom dress at this mall last year," Missy said. "She said it's the best place to shop."

"I love the specialty stores here. I'll take you to my favorite card shop. They have great notepads and rubber stamps. I've never been here when they have the Valentine's Day stuff out. I'll bet they've got neat stuff."

Once they were inside the mall, Barbara asked, "Do you need a snack right away, or do you want to shop first?"

"I'm okay," Missy said.

"Then let's check out the directory for the maternity shops. We could walk miles in this mall without stumbling onto one." They located the map. "Mommy To Be," Barbara read. "It's one level up."

The shop was midsized, with window displays that were both artful and tasteful. The manager of the shop, a stylish woman in her fifties, greeted them, introduced herself as Connie and offered assistance.

"We need to look at maternity bras," Barbara said.

"We have three basic styles," the woman said. "I'll be happy to show them to you." She took a tray from within a glass display counter and lifted a white cotton brassiere by its straps. "Many women who plan to nurse find it practical to buy our basic nursing bra to wear when they're pregnant. Then they don't have to buy separate maternity bras and nursing bras."

Missy stared quietly at the utilitarian undergarment.

"It's a little...plain," Barbara said, voicing the girl's obvious reaction.

Connie laughed. "It's not fancy, I'll admit. But the fabric doesn't hold moisture, and it provides strong support."

She replaced the first style and picked up another, this one with touches of lace trim. "This might be a better choice, though it's a bit pricier than the plain jane."

"And this one?" Barbara asked, touching the third bra on the tray. Beige instead of white, with satin appliqués and lace panels, it was much prettier and more delicate than the other two.

"This is lovely, isn't it? It's our most feminine bra, but it's not a nursing bra, which means a double expenditure if you plan to nurse." She looked pointedly at Barbara. "Are you planning to nurse, or are you still trying to decide?"

It was a natural assumption, Barbara reasoned frantically. Of course the woman would think it was she who was pregnant instead of Missy. Still, she felt her cheeks coloring in what had to be a visible flush, as the old, familiar ache of knowing she was not pregnant and probably never would be slowly filled her.

She tried not to sound shaken as she spread her arm across Missy's shoulders for support—physical support for herself, moral support for Missy—and told the clerk, "You're asking the wrong woman."

Connie registered surprise briefly, but quickly recovered. Shifting her gaze to Missy, she said lightly, "Either I'm getting old, or mothers are getting younger. Why don't we start by measuring you to see what size you need, then you can decide which style you want. You might want to check out our sale rack before going into the dressing room. I'll be in with my tape measure momentarily."

Missy selected a pair of jeans and a knit pantsuit from the rack, and then she and Barbara went into the dressing room. She tried on the jeans first.

"Those are great!" Barbara said. "They're a little long, but we can turn up a hem in nothing flat."

"May I come in?" Connie asked from the other side of the curtain door.

Barbara looked at Missy, who nodded, then pulled back the curtain to allow the clerk in. Connie was holding a tape measure. "Those fit you perfectly," she said, giving the jeans a once-over.

"My butt's getting big," Missy replied as she stood with her backside to the mirror and looked over her shoulder at her reflection.

"That's your body preparing for childbirth," Connie said. "Hormones cause the hip bones to move apart.

Your feet do the same thing. They get wider to distribute the extra weight. Isn't nature remarkable?"

*Remarkable. Oh, yes.* So remarkable that Barbara had to choke back the bitterness as she recalled her years of trying to conceive a child and the disappointment that she had been cheated out of the experience of carrying one. She'd wanted it so badly—the queasiness, the changes in her body, the feel of a child moving inside her, the pain and joy and wonder of birth, of a child drawing sustenance from her breast.

A glance at Missy's face and a glimpse of the confusion clouding Missy's eyes as Connie talked about the remarkable feats of nature brought Barbara crashing back to reality. Here was a scared teenager dealing with an unplanned pregnancy, disrupted lives, and a Solomonesque decision that had to be made.

She could not look at Missy without seeing Richard, could not meet Missy's desperate eyes without recalling the equivalent despair in Richard's. And she could not remember Richard without feeling an overwhelming surge of love for him. She loved him with all the intensity of the seventeen-year-old she'd been when he'd broken her heart and with all the sagacity of a thirty-four-year-old who'd been hurt and now approached life and love with caution and realistic expectations. And because she loved him so much, and because Missy was part of him—his blood—she loved Missy, too.

Connie was wrapping a tape measure around Missy's chest, just below her breasts. "I always insist on measuring," she said. "Women come in and tell me a bra size, without realizing that their breasts change drastically when . . . Did I pinch you, sweetie?"

"No," Missy said dazedly. She had such a strange expression on her face that Barbara poised to catch her in case she fainted.

"I felt something," she said, spreading her hand over her abdomen.

"A pain?" Connie asked, concerned, but cool as a cucumber. "Did it feel like a cramp?"

"No," Missy said. "It just—it was like something moved."

"The baby?" Barbara asked, unable to suppress her awe.

"I don't know," Missy said. "Maybe."

"How far along are you?" Connie asked, and when Missy didn't have a ready answer, added, "When are you due?"

"June," Missy and Barbara said in unison.

Connie counted back on her fingers. "That puts you at five months. It probably *is* the baby. You've never felt it before?"

"No. Oh!" Her hand flew back to her abdomen.

"Pain?" Barbara asked.

Missy shook her head. Wide-eyed, she said, "I think it *is* the baby moving."

"Do you think I'd be able to feel it, too?" Barbara asked, and Missy moved her hand.

"Was that it?" Barbara asked, truly excited. Missy nodded furiously. Then, slowly, their gazes met, and they both laughed aloud.

Sensing that she was intruding, Connie began rolling her tape measure. "I'll be at the counter if you need me."

As soon as she was gone, Barbara told Missy, "We're going to have to celebrate somehow."

Missy nodded, then spontaneously threw her arms around Barbara. "I'm glad we came shopping together."

"So am I," Barbara said, knowing that Missy wasn't referring to the shopping at all. She stroked the girl's back maternally. "So am I."

The poignant moment quickly dissolved as Missy drew away and began looking in the mirror again. "So," Barbara said, "are you going to take those jeans? How do they feel at the waist? Comfortable?"

Missy decided to buy both the jeans and the pantsuit, which had a top that looked more like the big shirts popular with teenagers than like a maternity garment.

Feeling triumphant over their shopping success, Barbara carried the garments to the counter while Missy changed back into her own clothes. As she waited, she noticed a display of books along the wall and perused the titles. One in particular drew her attention: *Pregnancy Week by Week*. Flipping through it, she was captivated by the in utero photographs of developing embryos.

"Do you have this book?" she asked when Missy returned from the dressing room.

Missy shook her head.

"I'd like to buy it for you. Would that be all right?"

Missy shrugged. "I guess so."

"Good." She put the book on the counter.

Connie had already folded the garments Missy was buying. "What did you decide about the bras?"

Chewing on her bottom lip, Missy turned helplessly to Barbara. Barbara smiled. "I rather like the pretty one."

Missy's relief was visible.

"How many and which colors?"

"Colors?" Missy and Barbara said in unison.

"The others are in white only, but this one comes in fleshtone beige, teal, coral rose and black."

"Why don't you show them to us?" Barbara suggested.

Missy looked at the colored undergarments with the intense concentration of a kid in a toy store. She touched the strap of the teal blue bra tentatively, as though afraid it might burn her. She seemed almost awed by it.

After an inordinate amount of time, when Missy still didn't appear close to a decision, Barbara suggested, "You're going to need several. Why not two of the beige and one each of two other colors?"

"Really?"

Barbara thought of something. "Your father didn't put you on a strict budget with the credit card, did he?"

"Uh-uh," Missy answered quickly. "He said if I went too hog wild the credit card people would quit approving the charges."

"I don't think we're anywhere near 'hog wild' yet," Barbara said, her heart filling a little when she thought how much like Richard the sentiment sounded. "So show the lady which colors you want."

After browsing through the other maternity shops and the maternity departments in several major stores,

Barbara and Missy decided to take a dinner break and then go to the card shop on their way out of the mall.

"If we'd bought one more thing, we wouldn't have fit into the booth with all these bags," Missy said after they'd ordered their food.

"We found such pretty things!" Barbara said. "They make such fashionable maternity clothes now, you can hardly tell them from regular clothes." She looked at Missy inquisitively. "Hey! Why the gloomy face all of a sudden? Don't you like your new clothes?"

"Heather's mom says when I start showing I can still visit Heather at her house, but Heather can't go anywhere with me in public."

Barbara tried not to overreact. "Have you and Heather been friends a long time?"

Missy nodded.

"Then what her mother's doing must hurt your feelings a lot."

Missy frowned sullenly. And then, almost explosively, she said, "It's not fair."

"No, it's not. And I'm sure she isn't trying to hurt you. She's just . . . parents are scared. All the time. And she's probably trying to protect Heather."

"She acts like Heather's a goody-goody and I'm a slut." Missy's bitterness showed.

"Up here—" Barbara pointed to her temple "—Heather's mother knows that you're not a slut. But that just makes her more afraid, because if you're not a slut and it happened to you, then it could just as easily happen to Heather. She just hasn't thought about how much she's hurting you."

Missy's expression remained sullen as the waiter placed their plates in front of them. Barbara waited for the young man to leave, then released a sigh as she picked up her fork. If Heather's mom had been within her reach at that moment, Barbara would cheerfully have stabbed her with the utensil. But, being the wise, mature person that she was, she corked her fuming temper and forced her voice to be calm. "I've always loved the Caesar salad here."

Being upset over Heather's mother apparently did nothing to quell Missy's appetite. Barbara watched her eat with a secret surge of maternal satisfaction, then urged her to have a scoop of ice cream for dessert while she herself had a cup of coffee. She almost choked on her coffee when Missy confessed, very somberly, "I've never had a colored bra before. Except beige. Grandmother said beige is okay."

"But she didn't like teal blue or coral rose?"

"She says colored underwear is inappropriate for young girls. It's too provocative."

Barbara felt sad inside, but she managed to smile. "Maybe your grandmother just hasn't noticed what a grown-up young lady you've become."

Soon she would, Barbara thought. Soon she would....

"HOW OLD IS YOUR MOTHER?" Barbara asked. It was Friday night. Missy had gone to the sneak preview of a new movie with her friends and was going to be staying for the regular showing of a second film. Richard had come to Barbara's bearing cartons of Chinese food and a video.

After eating, they'd watched about ten minutes of the movie before a cuddle led to a kiss and a kiss led to the bedroom, where they were now lying, basking in the afterglow of slow, sweet loving.

"She just turned seventy," Richard answered. "Why?"

"I remember her as being older than my mom. I just wondered if she really was, or if I just perceived her that way."

Richard pushed up on one elbow and looked down at her face. "Nice try."

"What do you mean?"

"I mean . . . that question didn't come out of thin air. You weren't just idly wondering."

"You're right. Something Missy said made it sound as if your mother might be a little more out of step with the times than a lot of grandmothers. I just wondered if age might be a factor."

"It's not just age. My mother's always been a little . . . out of step. She was an old maid, did you know that?"

Barbara shook her head.

"She never said so in so many words, but she was over thirty when she married, and you know what it must have been like in a small town back then. My father was almost twenty years older than her. A widower. She had several miscarriages before she had me. It must have astounded them both when she carried me to term."

He dropped back onto the pillow with a weary sigh. "It wasn't so bad when Missy was small, but when she started growing up, they started arguing about things like shaving her legs, using hair spray, clothes."

"And you were stuck in the middle."

"Yep. Usually defending Missy. When Heather— Missy's best friend—got her driver's license, it created real problems. My mother didn't think it was proper for girls to go out unescorted after dark. She had a dark, abiding fear that Missy might have inherited a wild streak from Christine."

"She didn't tell Missy that?" Barbara asked, appalled.

"Of course not. We never discussed Christine in front of Missy. Christine inflicted enough heartache on Missy without our adding to it. Missy knew she was a lousy mother. There was no reason she had to know what a lousy wife she was."

*But she knows*, Barbara thought, recalling Missy's curiosity about her mother. Deciding to change the subject, she rolled onto her stomach, stacked her hands palms down on his chest and propped her chin on the topmost hand so that her eyes met his. "Missy and I had a great shopping trip. What did you think of her new clothes?"

"The clothes were fine."

"We didn't spend too much, did we?" Barbara asked, sensing displeasure in his oddly clipped reply. "Missy said you didn't give her a dollar limit, and most of what we bought was on sale."

"You didn't spend too much."

"Then what's wrong?"

"What do you mean?"

"It's a simple enough question. If your jaw was clenched any tighter, I wouldn't be able to understand what you're saying. Obviously something about the shopping trip has your dander up."

"Do you really think that book was a good idea?"

"Book?" Barbara had to think a minute before she realized what he was talking about. "You mean the one on prenatal development?"

"That's the one. Do you think it was a good idea?"

"Of course I think it was a good idea. I wouldn't have bought it if I didn't think Missy would enjoy having it."

"Don't you think it's a little cruel under the circumstances?"

"Cruel? For her to know what's happening to the baby inside her body?"

"She might be better off not knowing."

"Better off? She has a right to know what's happening inside her."

"The baby she may be giving up for adoption," Richard reminded her. "The more attached she is to this baby, the harder it's going to be on her if she makes that decision."

Appalled and wounded, Barbara sat up abruptly, yanking the sheet over her breasts and anchoring it there with her arm. She glared at him. "She's already *attached* to the baby, Richard. It's a physical fact. They are *connected*, sharing oxygen and nutrients. Maybe you can't fully understand that, but—"

Richard sat up, too, propped his pillow against the headboard and settled back against it. He folded his arms over his waist belligerently. "Don't try to turn this into a male-female thing, Barbara. I simply meant that the less Missy focuses on the baby, the better off she's going to be if she decides to give the baby up."

"Well, it's not so simple, Mr. Voice of Logic! A woman who's pregnant doesn't just 'not focus' on the child she's carrying. Her mind may not be focusing, but her instincts are. Did she tell you that she felt her baby move?"

"No." His anger had waned, so his reply was soft.

"We were in the dressing room. She wasn't sure what it was at first, but it moved again, and we both felt it. Oh, Richard, you should have seen her face. The awe when that little bundle of life moved."

"You felt it, too?"

"Yes. She let me put my hand on her abdomen. It was a special moment. That's why I bought the book for her—as sort of a celebration of the baby moving."

With tenderness in his eyes, he reached out to cradle her face. "I know your intentions were good."

Barbara tensed. "My intentions were good, *but...?*"

"God, Barbara, don't you see what you're doing? You're treating Missy's pregnancy like a blessed event."

"Well, someone has to. Obviously you're not!"

"Well, excuse me for not stocking up on cigars and putting an announcement in the paper."

"No one's asking you for enthusiasm," she said stonily.

A charged silence followed. Finally, Barbara placed her hands on his arms and said intensely, "She's carrying a child, Richard."

"Yes. And you're so starry-eyed over the idea of pregnancy that you're blind to the bald reality of this particular situation."

"The bald reality?" Barbara echoed faintly, trying to make some kind of sense of his sudden animosity.

"This situation doesn't have any happy endings, Barbara. If she keeps the baby, her life is going to be centered around parenthood. If she stays in school, she's going to be exhausted from trying to take care of the baby and study at the same time. There won't be any time left for fun. No more sneak previews with her friends, that's for sure. And dating? Forget it. Guys are going to think she's a sure thing, but when it comes to commitment—who wants the baggage of a child?"

He quieted suddenly, as if embarrassed by the frenzy he'd worked himself into. His expression and tone turned defensive. "I know what I'm talking about. I've been there. Parenthood isn't all that pitter-patter of lit-tle feet and the joy-of-a-child's-smile crap."

"No one's saying it is," Barbara said. "I'm not trying to romanticize motherhood. I'm simply saying that Missy has a child growing inside her, and she has an instinctive attachment to it. The book I bought allows her to see what's happening to that life as it grows."

"Barbara, it's the kind of book a woman buys when she's thrilled about being pregnant. Every time Missy opens that book, she's going to feel a little closer to the baby. Can't you see that closeness is only going to make it harder on her if she decides to give the baby up?"

Bile rose in Barbara's throat and a hot flush colored her face as she suddenly realized that his point was valid. How could her judgment have been so flawed? She'd allowed herself to become so emotionally in-volved with Missy's reaction to feeling the baby move that she hadn't considered the impact the book might have on Missy.

Groaning, she turned away from him, hugging the sheet to herself.

"Barbara." Concerned, Richard extended his arm with the intention of comforting her, but he stopped short of actually touching her. Her naked back and shoulders were just too tempting.

Finally she spoke, softly. "I was afraid of this. I'm not qualified for a situation like this. I knew I didn't have the right experience, and I let good intentions cloud my judgment."

She twisted so she could see his face. "I thought I'd be able to help because I cared so much."

"You *have* helped Missy."

"A counselor's supposed to be objective. God, Richard, how could I possibly be objective about Missy when I'm sleeping with her father? When we have so much history together? If things had happened differently, she could have been mine."

The idea, finally voiced, hung in the air like a cloud of vapor, so compelling that it seemed to almost have substance. Barbara and Richard stared at each other in stunned silence until, shivering involuntarily, Barbara pulled the sheet closer around her. "I shouldn't have said that."

His gaze, sad and regretful, leveled with hers. "Do you think I haven't thought it? I was catching up on some paperwork at the house the other night and she brought me a peanut butter apple."

She was trembling, and this time Richard did touch her, capping her shoulders. The look in her eyes made him feel utterly helpless. "Look, Barbara, I probably overreacted about the book. Missy was thrilled with it. She was reading it when I went in to tell her good-night, the night you went shopping. She showed me a picture of a five-month fetus."

Barbara's voice was flat. "How did you respond?"

"How was I supposed to respond?" His frustration was evident. "I looked at the picture and said something like, 'That's interesting.'"

He could tell from her eyes that it wasn't what she'd been hoping for. "My heart was in my throat!" he said defensively. "All I could think of was how devastated she's going to be if she gives that baby away. And what a disastrous mess the baby will make of her life if she doesn't."

He let his hands slide down her arms. "I don't have any experience to draw on," he said. "The only pregnant woman I've had any dealings with was Christine, and she was always complaining about puking in the morning, feeling fat, getting stretch marks. She blamed me for everything, every little detail of the curse that had been visited upon her. If there hadn't been witnesses in the labor room, I think she would have killed me with her bare hands. We never got in an argument that she didn't throw it up to me what she'd been through because of me. And Missy."

"She blamed Missy?" Barbara asked, horrified.

Richard frowned at the uncomfortable memories he'd dredged up. "Yeah. Well, she didn't have any books about how babies develop, and she wouldn't have read them if someone had given her one. So you see, I don't have any experience with enthusiasm."

Barbara put her hand over his. "Next time try focusing on the fact that the baby developing inside Missy is your grandchild."

"My grandchild." He vented his pent-up frustration with a blistering swear word. "I'm thirty-six years old, and I haven't been young since I was nineteen! I'm not ready for a grandchild!"

Barbara leaned forward and slid her arms around his neck. A shuddering sigh vibrated through her as she hugged him, trying to absorb his anguish. "Grandchildren don't ask if you're ready."

They held each other for long minutes. Richard clung to her, wishing he knew how to tell her what she meant to him, what her friendship meant, her fierce loyalty. Gently he pushed her hair aside and kissed her neck, following it to her jaw, dropping a trail of kisses along the way to her face. "Your cheeks are wet," he said.

"My heart is breaking for you and Missy."

His arms tightened around her and he lay back, pulling her with him. He soothed her, stroking her hair, kissing the top of her head while her tears spilled onto his chest unabated.

The sheet had shifted, and her breasts pressed into his ribs. He folded his knee and draped his leg across hers possessively. Their closeness was not sexual; it was the embrace of two human beings who needed human contact, needed to mingle their troubled hearts, soothe each other's souls.

Minutes swelled into half an hour before either of them found the will to disrupt the silence. It was Barbara who spoke. "Have you and Missy talked about the baby?"

"I've helped her take care of everything so far. The doctor, the lawyer. You, when she applied for home study."

"It's obvious that you've taken care of business. The question was, have the two of you talked about the baby? About her choices, and the pros and cons of each."

Richard covered his face with his hands and sighed. "No. Okay? I'll admit it. We haven't had a specific talk! If that makes me a bad father or unsupportive, I'm sorry."

"I wasn't criticizing you."

"I've had enough trouble just dealing with the fact that she's pregnant. I haven't moved far enough beyond that to think about a baby. Up to this point it's been an abstract. Maybe it *is* a male-female thing. I've been caught up in the complications having a child would entail, and she's reading books about prenatal development."

"It's a parent thing more than a gender thing," she said. "You're looking at long-term ramifications and Missy's more involved in the immediate situation. That's typical."

She pushed up on one elbow so that she could see his face. "You and she need to talk and work out some 'what if' scenarios."

"What if?"

"What would happen if she kept her baby? What would happen if she gave it up? It's very reassuring to detail options. It's like knowing that whatever happens, you'll be prepared instead of surprised."

"What kind of details should we discuss?"

"The more specific, the better. Where would a baby sleep? What are the child care options while Missy is at school? What responsibilities would you expect Missy to assume in terms of supporting the baby? How would having a baby influence her choice of colleges?"

He was looking at her strangely. "What?" she asked.

"You're remarkable," he said. "Just zip, boom, pop, and you've got a list of questions."

She smiled, pleased that she had impressed him. "It's part of my job. You could probably zip, boom and pop me information about financing a house or which end of town offers the best elementary schools." She paused. "How did the subject of adoption come up?"

Richard shook his head. "To be honest, I hadn't even thought that far before the attorney who prepared the surrender papers for the father said that if the father signed, it would clear the way for Missy to put the child up for adoption. He said people call him all the time looking for newborns and that if Missy—" He swallowed. "When I told her what he'd said, Missy said her doctor had told her the same thing."

"Ironic, isn't it? So many girls pregnant when they don't want to be, and so many women yearning for children they can't have. Doctors and lawyers arrange adoptions like stockbrokers selling over-the-counter stocks."

"The lawyer said there's a long waiting list for healthy white infants through public agencies."

"Years," Barbara said, then searched Richard's eyes. "You think it's the best option for Missy, don't you?"

He pondered the question before replying. "Missy would have her life back, some couple would have a baby they truly want, and the baby would have a loving home. It *sounds* so tidy."

"Very tidy—until you consider the emotional element."

Richard drew in a deep breath and released it. "Yeah. The emotional element."

Barbara caressed his cheek with her fingertips, then kissed him briefly on the mouth. "You'll get through this, Richard. Missy will, too."

She settled her cheek in the crook of his shoulder and snuggled closer to him.

Richard stroked her hair, savoring its silky texture. "You're not making it easy for me to peel myself off this mattress and leave."

"Why would you want to do a ridiculous thing like that?"

His breath fanned through her hair, tickling her scalp deliciously. "When we were dating," he said tenderly, "and we were both virgins, I used to lie awake nights aching for you and imagining what it would be like to be inside you. Now I lie awake missing you and wishing I could go to sleep knowing you'll be in bed next to me in the morning."

He waited for her to say something, but she remained profoundly silent. He was still stroking her hair. The scent of it, clean and female, soothed him. "Do you know what I decided halfway through that first sleepless night after we made love?"

"What?" she murmured, wiggling just a bit, giving him a new awareness of all the places their bodies were touching.

"That I want you to sleep in my bed with me every night, so I can wake up with you every morning for the rest of my life."

Again, she was strangely quiet. Richard waited. And waited. Until, finally, in a voice too soft even to be called a whisper, she said, "Aren't you supposed to kiss a woman after you say something like that to her?"

Richard pushed up on his elbow and looked down at her face. "You know that kissing you is my second most favorite thing in the universe," he said, "but don't you think I deserve some reaction to my proposal first?"

"Was that a proposal?" Barbara teased. "I thought you just wanted to live in sin."

"Don't joke about this, Barbara. I've never been more serious in my life. I'm not very good at sin. All my experiences with sin have been disastrous. I want the real thing this time. The right thing, with the right woman. Don't you—I thought—don't you feel the same way?"

She didn't reply. Finally he said frantically, "Say something, Barbara. Don't you love me? Doesn't it mean something to you when we're together like this?"

Barbara closed her eyes and sighed, then reopened them, fixing her gaze on Richard. "Of course it does. You've made me feel seventeen again. It's impossible for me to look at you and not remember all the intensity of the love I felt for you back then. And the chemistry between us is—there were times at night that I used to lie awake, remembering your kisses, and fear that I'd die without ever finding out what it would be like to make love with someone who could make me feel so much."

Richard shook his head in mute denial of what she was suggesting. He couldn't be as mistaken about the nature of their relationship as she suggested. He knew it when she touched him. He knew it when he looked into her eyes. He knew it beyond reason or need of explanation; he knew it was not only in his mind, but his heart and his very soul.

"This isn't—*nostalgia*," he said. "It's not let's-get-one-on-for-old-time's-sake. I love you, Barbara. And I dare you to look me square in the eye and tell me you don't love me."

"But you're talking about a lifelong commitment when we've only seen each other—what, three times? four?—after seventeen years of total estrangement. You're in the middle of a major crisis, Richard. You shouldn't be making any decisions about your own life when you're so caught up in Missy's dilemma. You could be holding on to me because of what I represent—youth and innocence and the blind optimism that go along with them."

"You don't believe that any more than I do," he said. "Can't you drop the counselor crap for a while and just let yourself feel something without analyzing it to death?"

Her response was immediate. She sat up, pulling the sheet with her, holding it in place like armor. "The counselor crap? I'm a little more cautious than you, and like to think things through a little more thoroughly, and that's 'counselor crap'? I hate to bring it up, but you haven't had great results from your policy of rushing into things blindly."

"This is different, Barbara. This is you and me. Not Christine. Not the woman I was screwing on the couch when Missy walked in. I loved you seventeen years ago and I fouled that up. I still love you, and I don't want anything to foul it up this time. We've wasted half our lives. We don't have any more time to waste on half-ass commitments."

The expression on her face was unreadable. "Well, say something!" he said after what seemed an inordinate period of silence.

She rolled her eyes in taxed exasperation. "Is that supposed to knock me off my feet? You want to get married because we don't have any more time to waste on half-ass commitments?"

Richard frowned in pure frustration. "Okay. So I'm not romantic. Do I get any points at all for sincerity?"

Barbara shook her head.

"How about for being madly, hopelessly in love with you and thinking you're the sexiest woman alive and wanting to spend the rest of my life with you?"

Barbara smiled and asked in a sultry drawl, "If kissing me is your second favorite thing in the universe, what's your first?"

Richard's hungry gaze slid over her bed-rumpled hair, her face, her bare shoulders. "I'm not sure I can show you in just—" he glanced at the clock "—twenty minutes."

"You could try," she challenged, letting the sheet drop.

## 10

HOLDING THE TELEPHONE receiver to her ear, Barbara gave Missy a reassuring smile as she waited for Richard to answer his office line. "Mr. Benson, this is Barbara Wilson."

"Barbara? Why so formal?"

"That's right. Missy's counselor."

"She's with you, isn't she?"

"Yes. She's right here. We've been having a nice visit."

"As nice as our last visit was?"

Barbara steeled herself against the suggestion in his voice. "In fact, something's come up in our discussion that I wanted to talk to you about. Missy tells me that the doctor is going to do an ultrasound at her next visit, and she's a little apprehensive about it."

Richard was instantly concerned. "It's not painful, is it? Or dangerous?"

"No. But medical machinery can be a little intimidating. Mr. Benson, she's asked if I would go with her, and I told her I'd have to talk to you about it first."

"Do you want to go?"

"I think it's an excellent idea. But naturally, I felt we should ask your opinion."

"If it's what Missy wants and you don't mind, I'm all for it."

Barbara gave Missy a thumbs-up and forced a smile. "I'm so glad you feel that way, Mr. Benson."

"I want to talk to you about this. Alone. When Missy isn't listening in."

"I agree," Barbara said evenly. "That would be a good idea."

"Tonight?"

"Yes. Missy and I are having a great visit. We've been making spaghetti sauce." She paused as Missy waved frantically. "Excuse me."

"Tell him I'll make him spaghetti now that I know how."

"Don't you want to tell him yourself?"

Missy shook her head. "That's okay. You can tell him for me."

Barbara relayed the message, listened, then laughed. "Yes. I'll tell her that."

After hanging up the phone, she turned to Missy. "He said that if the spaghetti is half as good as the pot roast was, he's going to hire you out as a chef."

"Daddy's so silly sometimes," Missy said, but Barbara could see the pleasure her father's compliment had given her.

That evening, Richard brought wine to go with the spaghetti. "Good," Barbara said when he presented her with the bottle. "We may need it."

Concern captured Richard's features. "I could tell by your voice that something was bothering you. Is it this doctor's visit with Missy?"

"It's everything," Barbara said. "If you're not too hungry, why don't we talk before we eat?"

Richard nodded.

"Make yourself comfortable, then," Barbara said. "I'll put this in the refrigerator."

When she returned to the living room, he was sitting on the couch. He patted the space next to him, and she sat as he'd invited.

"Don't I even get a hello kiss?" he asked.

"Oh, Richard," she said, gladly going into his proffered embrace. They hugged long after the kiss ended.

"Does this have anything to do with the fact that I asked you to marry me?" he asked. "By the way, that was pretty sneaky, enticing me to make love to you so you could avoid talking about it. You knew I had to leave."

"So did you," she said. "And you weren't exactly fighting me off."

"I'm not perfect, but I'm not crazy, either. You obviously weren't in the mood for talk, and you do have incredible breasts." He grinned unforgivably at the blush that colored her cheeks.

Barbara stiffened her spine. "This time, we talk."

"First," he said. "Then I can show you how much I missed you since Friday night."

Barbara fought the curl of desire his suggestive bantering brought to life inside her. "We've got some serious problems to discuss, Richard," she said firmly.

He nodded solemnly. "About Missy, or about us?"

"About Missy. And about us. Oh, Richard, I feel so incredibly conflicted. When we decided to keep our relationship between us, it seemed so simple and logical. I thought you were right about Missy having enough on her mind without us throwing a serious relationship in her face. I still think so, but—"

She paused and wiped her hand over her face. "It was hard enough when it was just a matter of your having to sneak over here like a married man, but the closer I get to Missy, the more I feel we're deceiving her as much as protecting her. When I was talking to you on the phone in front of her, it was like lying."

"So you think we should level with her about our relationship?"

"I don't know," she admitted miserably. "Since you asked me to marry you, I've been more confused than ever."

"About us?"

He wasn't expecting her to melt. But that's the only way he could have described the way everything about her softened as she looked at him. "I used to sit in class and practice writing Barbara Simmons Benson. That should make me question whether my feelings are real or just memories of old feelings that were never resolved. But it doesn't."

Her eyes held love as she smiled bittersweetly. "I don't know if I never stopped loving you or if I just fell in love all over again. I just know that I'm crazy in love with you."

A thousand-ton weight floated from Richard's chest. He'd known she loved him, known it with every fiber of his being, but it was a relief to hear her admit it. He cradled her head, sliding his fingers into her hair and curving them around her scalp. His face hovered an inch from hers. "Say it," he said.

"I love you?" she replied, caught off guard by his intensity.

"That's old news." His mouth was so close to hers that his lips brushed hers when he smiled before imploring, "Now say, 'Yes.'"

He swallowed the word as it came out of her mouth, feeding on its significance. He wouldn't have expected that after all their lovemaking of the past weeks, that a single kiss would carry so much meaning. But this kiss, which started with a promise, became a covenant between them. It left them breathless and jubilant and complete in a way they'd never been complete before.

"It's official now," Richard said.

"Yes," she said, putting her head on his shoulder. After a long hesitation, she said, "We'll never have just this moment again. I wish . . . that we could put it in a bottle and take it out when there's nothing hanging over our heads to spoil it."

"Missy?"

Barbara nodded. "The omission is so much bigger now than when we were just exploring what would happen if we got to know each other again."

"She'll be pleased, Barbara. She likes you."

"And she loves you. She trusts both of us. Which is why she could feel betrayed when she finds out that we kept this from her."

"You think it's time to tell her about us?"

"I think it's time to think about the best time and the best way."

"Maybe if we did it slowly, if you came to the house to visit. Missy would like that. I could mention that I find you attractive. She'd probably suggest that I—"

"And what if she reacts negatively to the idea because she's scared it would threaten her relationship with you? Would we call it quits? Or would we sneak around some more?"

"We're not sneaking around, damn it!" Richard said. "We're being discreet to protect my daughter when she's got enough on her mind without our springing this on her, too."

"You were right. You wanted to wait until Missy's crisis was resolved before we got so deeply involved. If I hadn't thrown myself at you—"

He cupped her chin and tilted it until he could see her face. "You didn't throw yourself at me. We were like two locomotives charging toward each other on the same track."

"You're sweet to remember it that way."

"I don't regret a minute—not even a second—of the time we've spent together. The frustration is in all the years we wasted and can't get back again. This thing with Missy will eventually work itself out, and when it does—"

"Maybe she'll be my maid of honor."

The look in his eyes was hot enough to melt stone. "I'd marry you this minute if there was a preacher standing in front of us to perform the ceremony."

Barbara hugged him fiercely, and for a few minutes, at least, they lived only in the moment, savoring the richness of being able to hold each other after having been separated so many years.

A fit of barking from the apartment next door shattered the spell. "Someone's doorbell is ringing," Barbara observed idly.

"How do they put up with that dog?"

"Gizmo? He's a cutie! He just hates doorbells."

Richard harrumphed skeptically. After a silence, he asked apprehensively, "Tell me about this test Missy's going to have."

"I'm no expert," she said. "But a sonogram is something like radar. It uses sound waves that bounce off solid objects and create images. There's no pain involved. Not every expectant woman has one, but Missy's pregnancy is considered high risk because of her age."

"She didn't tell me that. About the high risk. Is she— could she be in physical jeopardy?"

"I'm not a doctor."

"But you're a woman. A smart woman."

"My opinion? Missy's a healthy sixteen-year-old. She and the baby will be fine. If she were fourteen, with a history of drug abuse or malnutrition or heavy smoking, the prognosis wouldn't be as good for either, especially the baby." She gave Richard an inquiring look. "Why haven't you asked Missy's doctor all these questions?"

"I haven't met Missy's doctor."

"You've taken her for her appointments."

"I sit in the waiting room and write the checks. It's an OB-GYN office. They've never asked me into the treatment rooms or whatever is behind that door the nurse takes the patients through."

"And you haven't asked to go?"

"It's a woman's world back there, and I don't want to invade Missy's privacy. And don't give me that look!"

"What look?"

"That you're-an-insensitive-male-and-uncaring-father look!"

"That wasn't what I was thinking at all," Barbara said.

"If she'd asked, I would have gone with her."

"Do you honestly think I'd have agreed to marry you if I'd thought you were insensitive or uncaring?"

Richard frowned in frustration. "No. I'm sorry. My fuse is a little short. I just...I feel so responsible and yet so...powerless."

"You're a parent."

"Sometimes I don't feel like much of one."

Barbara stroked his back soothingly. "It takes a caring parent with a keen sense of responsibility to achieve the level of frustration you're at."

He turned and reflexively pulled Barbara into his arms. "If I'm so caring and sensitive, why didn't she tell me about this sonogram? Why didn't she ask me to go with her instead of—"

"Instead of me?"

Richard released a labored sigh. "Do I sound like an ungrateful jerk?"

Barbara smiled reassuringly. "We agreed that Missy needed a female confidante. That's why I suggested counselling."

"So you think this is one of those female bonding things?"

"As opposed to a rejection of you, yes. If the father were involved with the baby, she'd probably want him along, but she'd probably be a little self-conscious lying on a table with her belly bare in front of you. She's already embarrassed about being pregnant."

"She's embarrassed with me, and wouldn't be with the little twerp who got her pregnant?"

"It's not that simple. I said if the father were involved with the baby, she'd probably want him along. If that were the case, and Missy were older and married, you wouldn't think a thing about her wanting her husband with her."

"I guess."

"There just aren't many established rules for unmarried teenaged girls who are carrying babies the father couldn't care less about. It would be simpler if there were, so we could turn to Section 3-C on page thirty-seven of the rule book to find out who's supposed to go with Missy when she has a sonogram."

She patted Richard's knee. "That wine should be cool by now. Why don't you decant us a glass while I cook the spaghetti."

"'Decant'?" he repeated with a chuckle as they rose.

"Oh, all the best wine servers decant, don't you know?" she replied in a heavy, affected British accent.

"Glad I sprang for a bottle with a cork," he said drolly. "I'd hate to try to decant a screw-on."

Barbara put the water on to boil and then sat down at the table and picked up the glass of wine Richard had poured for her. She took a sip. It was robust and tart. "This was a good idea."

"I have some of those occasionally."

His hand was on the table, next to his glass, and she covered it with hers and gave it a gentle squeeze. "Probably a lot more often than you realize."

He responded with a small smile.

"I have an idea I want to run past you now," she said, trying to sound upbeat.

Richard's mouth curled sardonically. "If you waited until I had wine to bring it up, it can't be pleasant."

"It's not unpleasant," Barbara said. "It's just something to think about."

Richard groaned. "I don't want to think any more. Let's go to your bedroom and have mindless sex instead."

Barbara grinned drolly. "Later. First I want to feed you so you'll have enough energy to keep up with me. And while we're waiting for the water to boil, we might as well toss around some ideas."

"You'd be perfect if you weren't so damned clever," Richard grumbled.

"I'm serious, Richard."

"I know," he said resignedly. "Let's hear it."

"Physically, this test Missy's going to have is not going to be much, but it could have an enormous psychological impact. She'll actually be able to see an image of her baby moving on a screen, and she'll probably be given a printout of the baby's image."

"What? Like a computer printout?"

"Exactly. Only it looks like a black-and-white photo. Richard, some mothers frame these printouts, or post them someplace where they'll see them often."

"The baby's going to be a lot more real to her."

Barbara nodded. "If the baby's turned the right way, she may find out whether it's a boy or a girl."

Richard buried his face in his hands and swore, then sucked in a ragged breath. "How's she going to deal with this?"

"I'd say that depends a lot on how *you* deal w

"I'm not ready for this."

"It's here, and it's happening, whether you're re
for it or not. You're thirty-six. Missy's sixteen.
going to need your strength. Whether you thin
have the strength or not, she needs to believe that
have it. And if you can't find it, you're going to have
do a damn good job of faking it."

The water was boiling. She got up and put the noodles in, then stirred them. When she turned abruptly
to return to the table, she was startled to find Richard
right behind her. An involuntary shriek of surprise rose
from her throat.

He draped his arms over her shoulders and looked
into her eyes. "If I find the strength to handle this, it'll
be because you showed me where to look for it."

"We're not going to have to dig very deep to find it,"
she said soothingly.

## 11

MISSY GASPED involuntarily as the first gloop of ultra-sound transmission gel plopped onto her abdomen, then giggled nervously.

"Hey, it's not even cold!" the technician teased. "I have a special heater for it right over here."

Missy nodded. "It's okay. It just felt kinda wet."

"Well, you've survived the most traumatic part of the entire procedure," the technician said. "Now all you have to do is relax while we take a look at that baby."

*All she has to do is relax*, Barbara thought, saddened by the irony of it. If only Missy could relax, and have her dilemma miraculously resolved, her youth given back to her, her choices reduced to which dress to wear to the prom and which college to apply to.... If only she could relax, and she would no longer have to face making a decision that would challenge the emotional well-being of even the most stable adult. If only she could relax, and she would be a wonderfully normal teenager, with wonderfully normal teenage concerns, and her father could go to her and say, "Barbara and I are in love and we're going to be married and the three of us can be a family."

The technician, a dark-haired man in his early thirties, competently slid the smooth head of the sonogram transducer into the thickest puddle of transmitting gel and moved it back and forth to spread the gel evenly over her skin. His lively brown eyes reflected kindness as he asked, "Do you want me to point out everything as I go along?"

Missy looked at Barbara and, for a split second, Barbara knew with clarity and incisive acuity what it was like to be a parent and have a child turn to her expecting answers to impossible questions. What did Missy really want from her? Encouragement? Moral support? Did she secretly hope Barbara would discourage her from looking at the monitor so she wouldn't have to face the reality of the child inside her?

Barbara forced a benign smile. "It's up to you, sweetheart."

Was it relief that flitted across that heartrendingly young face as she turned to the technician and nodded? Had she been asking permission? Barbara couldn't tell. But she could see Missy's teeth worrying her bottom lip and caught the slight quiver in Missy's chin as she watched the image of her unborn child come into focus on the monitor.

"Look at that nice, steady heartbeat," the technician said. "Uh-oh. He's getting active now. Look at that leg action. This kid thinks he's a soccer player. Do you feel him kicking you?"

"Yeah," Missy said, her features expressing a blend of surprise, awe and concentration. She had been holding Barbara's hand loosely, and her fingers tightened around Barbara's as she concentrated on linking internal sensations to the electronic image.

"Oh!" Missy chortled as the baby made a strong and sudden kick that was especially pronounced. With a smile still lingering, she looked at Barbara as if to ask, Did you see that?

"If it's a girl, she's a candidate for the Rockettes," Barbara said.

"I'm going to try to get a close look at the baby's face. Let's see what we can see. There it is."

Missy's fingers tightened around Barbara's. "It has a nose."

Tears stung Barbara's eyes as she, like Missy, stared transfixed at the monitor. "It's a beautiful little face," she said. "A perfect face."

"I'm taking a picture now," the technician said. "Oops! We've embarrassed him. The little tyke must be camera shy. Let's see what else we can find."

Arms, legs—he scanned them individually, patiently waiting for the baby to turn in the right direction. "Now, if he'll just turn a little bit this way, we might be able to tell— Aha! The little fellow is pretty proud of himself. Look at that."

"It's a boy?" Missy asked.

"In my professional opinion, that's no shadow. I'm ninety-nine percent sure this little fellow's a boy." He grinned. "I have to leave a one-percent possibility for error so you don't sue me if it turns out to be a girl. I'm going to take another picture now, then we'll quit all this sight-seeing and get down to business."

Missy looked at Barbara. "It's a boy."

"It sure is," Barbara said.

The technician took measurements from various angles for another quarter of an hour. When he had to press the transducer until the pressure was uncomfortable, Missy squeezed Barbara's hand and bore the discomfort stoically. Her eyes never left the monitor. Nor did Barbara's.

"Everything looks fine," the technician said with an air of finality. "Let's try one more time to get a picture of that face. Good. Good. That's good. Okay, fellow, just turn a little bit this way and say 'Cheese.' Excellent."

He turned to Missy with a beaming smile. "He's very cooperative. We got a good shot that time. Now—" He pulled several tissues from a box on his supply table. "You can clean the goop off your belly, then go back across the hall and get dressed. The nurse will take you in to talk to Dr. Scofield after I've had a chance to show her what we've been up to."

The doctor was a petite woman with gray-tinged auburn hair pulled into a ponytail at her nape. She was friendly, but reserved. She shook Barbara's hand firmly when Missy introduced her. "I'm glad Missy was able to bring a friend today."

She reiterated essentially the same thing the technician had said. The baby appeared healthy and normal, with a strong heartbeat. The pictures the technician had given her were on her desk and she looked down at them, then smiled at Missy. "It's a boy."

Missy nodded self-consciously.

The doctor leaned back in her chair, commanding their attention with her authoritative demeanor. She spoke next as a physician, with professional detachment. "Have you read the literature I gave you?"

Chewing on her bottom lip, Missy nodded.

"Are you still considering adoption as an option?"

Missy shifted uncomfortably and averted her eyes. "Maybe."

The doctor drew in a deep breath and released it. She looked at Barbara, telling her, silently, that though she could not become emotionally involved, she acknowledged what her young patient was going through. "You'd have no problem at all placing a healthy baby boy."

Missy shrugged. She was still gnawing her bottom lip. And she was still not looking at the doctor.

"You still have some time to think about it," Scofield said. "But if you should want to meet some prospective parents—just to talk about it—it can be arranged. You wouldn't have to tell them your name just to talk."

Dr. Scofield glanced down at the pictures of the baby pensively. "Do you want these? I can put them in your file if you'd prefer. You could ask for them at any time."

"I want them," Missy murmured. The doctor slid them across the desk and Missy picked them up.

"Well, unless you have any questions, we're through for today."

Missy had no questions. A few minutes later she and Barbara were in Barbara's car. "That was sort of exciting," Barbara said.

Missy, still subdued, grunted, "Mmm-hmm."

"I feel like we should celebrate, don't you?" Barbara asked.

"Celebrate?"

"Seeing your baby's face."

Missy looked down at the pictures on her lap.

"It's still early," Barbara persisted. She wasn't comfortable taking Missy home without talking to her awhile. "Why don't we...go to the mall and look around a bit, and then go out for dinner? You can call your dad when we get to the mall and ask if it's all right."

"Okay."

They rode on in silence for a few minutes before Missy asked abruptly, "Why do so many people want baby boys?"

Talk about questions out of left field! Barbara considered the question before attempting to answer it. "People want children for a lot of reasons, Missy. Some of those reasons come from deep inside, from instincts that are as old as the human race. One of those instincts is to perpetuate themselves. Do you know what that means?"

"Sort of."

"It means that after they die, part of them will go on living through their children, and their children's children, and so on. And most men like to have a son to keep the family name alive, especially if it's an unusual name."

Missy's voice was expressionless as she said, almost as if thinking aloud, "My dad probably would have liked a boy better."

"Why ever would you think that?" Barbara asked.

Missy shrugged.

"All men think they want boys," Barbara said. "That's because men like to feel they're in control all the time, and they understand boys. They think all they have to do to raise a boy is buy baseballs. They feel totally helpless with little girls."

She chanced a sideways glance at Missy and was delighted to see a grin twitching on the girl's mouth. Encouraged, she continued. "Want to know a secret?"

Missy nodded cautiously.

"The first time a daddy holds a baby girl, he's scared to death. Because she's tiny and she's female—which means she's a total mystery to him. But something magical happens when a little girl wraps her fingers around her daddy's finger and squeezes it. There's a special bond there, a special way that daddies feel about little girls." She smiled at Missy. "You're your daddy's little girl, Missy. He might wonder what it would be like to have a son. Most men do. But he wouldn't want a son instead of you."

She couldn't tell if Missy was convinced, but the opportunity for heavy-duty talk had passed, at least until dinner. They had reached the mall.

They went straight to a kiosk of pay phones. Barbara handed Missy a quarter and walked over to a store window to stare idly at a display of kitchen gadgets while Missy called home. The next time she glanced Missy's way, the girl was waving frantically for her attention. She ran.

Missy put her hand over the mouthpiece of the receiver. "Daddy says he hasn't had dinner and he's hungry and he can meet us here in thirty minutes, but only if that's okay with you."

Barbara was assailed by a dozen emotions at once. What was Richard thinking? She and Richard and Missy having dinner together? "Tell him . . . of course. It's a great idea! I don't know why we didn't think of it."

Later, she wondered why she hadn't. The evening was a poignant glimpse into what their lives might eventually be. It seemed so natural to be in that informal restaurant with Richard and Missy, having dinner like any ordinary family on an outing to the local mall. It was so *right* to be there, encouraging Missy to tell Richard about the sonogram, secretly holding Richard's hand under the table for moral support as Missy showed him the blue booties they'd bought for the baby, exchanging secret smiles and nods the way parents would in a time of shared crisis.

For the hour and a half they spent in the restaurant, Barbara felt as though reality had meshed with her dream. She'd never felt closer to either of them than when Richard cajoled Missy into ordering apple cobbler with ice cream and then annoyed her by snitching bites of it. Their affection for each other, their closeness, their comfortable familiarity was so apparent in their bantering and teasing that Barbara felt the sting of tears as she watched them together, temporarily oblivious to the crisis that weighed so heavily on both their shoulders.

It was difficult to say goodbye, hugging Missy and telling her how much it meant to her to have been a part of the sonogram, then shaking Richard's hand and thanking him formally for the dinner instead of hugging him and telling him how much the evening had meant to her.

She went home feeling, at the same time, fulfilled and empty. Missy had needed her, and she'd been there for the girl. But she could not go home with Missy and Richard. As much as she loved them both, she was still, officially, only a counselor and confidante to Missy and a mistress to Richard. She was not yet family, neither wife nor mother, nor even stepmother.

As she climbed into bed—alone except for the latest issue of her favorite magazine—that deficiency in her relationship with Richard and his daughter loomed large in her mind. She was reading the magazine when the doorbell rang. Gizmo was barking wildly by the time she pulled on her terry robe and went to the door to peer through the peephole.

"I need you," Richard said, and she was in his arms even before the door clicked shut behind him. He'd never kissed her with such ferocity. He carried her to the bedroom and fell onto the bed with her, still kissing her. Then he took her with a driving urgency that would have been frightening if it hadn't been so thrilling. Afterward, as they lay together, heated, heaving and drained, he clung to her, covering her, arms encircling her, legs locked with hers.

"You knew," he said. "You knew and you prepared me."

Barbara wasn't thinking as clearly as she might have under less intense circumstances. "What'd I know?"

"That I was less prepared to deal with Missy's baby becoming a reality than Missy was."

"Oh, Richard," she said. "I wish I were as wise as you think I am. The truth is, I just warned you so you'd be prepared to support Missy."

Richard exhaled a ragged sigh. "Mother would never allow Missy to post things on the refrigerator the way her friends did, so we have this plastic frame, one of those box-type things, that we always put her latest awards or certificates in. Tonight she asked if we could put the pictures of her baby in that frame."

"Oh, Richard." It seemed so inadequate, but it was all Barbara could think of to say as she hugged him.

"She showed me a face, and she showed me a miniature baby and pointed out the penis. Jeez, Barbara. She showed me my grandson's face."

Seconds passed before he could speak again. "It was so ludicrous. She's still—I know she's not a child, but she's not an adult, either. Pictures of a baby don't belong in the plastic frame where you put perfect attendance certificates and spelling tests with smiley faces on them."

"What time is it?" Barbara asked abruptly.

"About eleven."

"Get dressed then. If we hurry, we can make it."

Richard didn't question her order. He was up and pulling on his underwear before he thought to ask where they were going.

"The drugstore down the street is open until midnight. I saw just what we need the last time I took film in to be processed."

Half an hour later in the checkout line, Richard looked at the ceramic picture frames he held in his hands. Both were baby blue. One had Baby written across the top in an alphabet block motif, and the second had a boy's worn sneakers in one bottom corner and a baseball and glove in the other. "There was a time I would have asked if you thought this was a good idea, but I'm not second-guessing your judgment anymore."

"She wanted the pictures, Richard. I was there. And she wanted them in the place that had always showcased her achievements." Her gaze met his. "I'm just glad you responded positively when she showed them to you."

"Attila the Hun couldn't have been unresponsive when she pointed to that tiny face."

"When you give her these frames, it's going to be a validation of the fact that you know she's carrying a child. She needs that, Richard. With the father totally uninvolved, and your mother off in Europe, you're all she has."

"That's not true," Richard said somberly. "She has you, too."

"Tonight—it was almost like—"

"I know," Richard agreed. "I felt it, too. A sense of family. A couple of times I felt like just blurting out that I loved you."

"Part of me wishes you had. But the rest of me knows Missy needed tonight to be just the way it was." She smiled. "It was so wonderfully ordinary. You and she were so relaxed with each other."

"It was like old times."

"And when you got home, she felt comfortable enough to show you the pictures."

They paid for the frames and drove back to Barbara's apartment. The interior of the car was dimly lit by the porch lights above the doors on the building in front of them. Barbara turned to Richard. "It's late. You don't have to get out."

"Yes, I do," he said, and then, more gently, "I know you have school tomorrow, so I won't stay but a few minutes. But, please—I need to hold you awhile longer before I go home."

Barbara smiled, her face luminous in the pale light. "I'd gladly sacrifice a night's sleep if you could hold me till morning."

He held her until she went to sleep, then tucked the covers around her and kissed her good-night before leaving. As he left, he checked the door to make sure the lock had engaged firmly.

For several seconds, he kept his hand on the knob.

"It won't be this way forever," he vowed aloud, but the only living thing that heard was the dog barking in her neighbor's apartment. As he walked away, he felt as though he were leaving a large chunk of his heart behind with her.

# 12

SOMETHING WAS VERY WRONG. Barbara knew it the instant Missy arrived for her Tuesday visit. Emotional strain was written in Missy's taut features, in her lethargic movements, in the sag of her shoulders and her reluctance to look Barbara in the eye as they conversed—if their terse exchange of rote phrases could even be defined as conversation.

"Would you like a glass of milk?" Barbara offered. "Or a peanut butter apple?"

Missy declined with a shake of her head. Looking at the forlorn young woman, Barbara found it difficult to reconcile this Missy with the teenager who'd been playfully sparring with her father over spoonfuls of apple cobbler less than a week before.

"Are you feeling all right?" Barbara asked, although her instincts told her that this dramatic transformation was more than a hormone-influenced mood swing associated with pregnancy. Missy's moroseness came from a troubled heart.

"I'm okay," Missy grumbled with a pitiable attempt at a shrug.

"You don't seem so chipper today," Barbara pressed. "Is there something on your mind? Something you'd like to talk over?"

For close to a minute, Missy was still as stone. Her bottom lip was between her teeth, and Barbara worried that she might actually draw blood. She fought a strong impulse to gather the troubled child into her arms and rock her, but she forced herself to wait for Missy to respond.

"I've got some papers I need to put together," she said, rising. "Do you mind if I work on them while we talk?"

Missy registered no objection, so Barbara spread three stacks of papers on the coffee table then sat down, Indian-style, on the floor in front of it to work. "The copy machine that collates has been broken all week," she said. "So I have to do these the old-fashioned way."

"I could help," Missy offered with more animation than she'd shown since her arrival.

"Great!" Barbara said. "One of us can stack and the other can staple." She got up and went to the desk and returned quickly with a stapler and a box of staples. "Are you any good at loading these things? I can't ever remember where the release button is."

"I can do it," Missy said.

Within minutes they had a routine established, with Missy stapling the sets Barbara collated. "You'll get one of these in your homeroom next week," Barbara said. "It's about the preliminary college admission exams. You'll want to sign up for them. They'll give you some idea how you might do on the real tests next year."

Missy grunted noncommittally.

"You're planning on going to college, aren't you?"

"I wanted to go to Florida State, but—" She frowned forlornly.

"There are some excellent colleges within commuting distance," Barbara said.

Missy's chin quivered. "Do you think I should give my baby up for adoption?"

Barbara moved to the couch and put her arms around Missy. "That's a big decision, Missy. You're going to have to give it a lot of thought."

"It's probably best for everybody."

It was a good response, logical and well thought out. Too good. Too pat.

"Have you been talking this over with anyone?" Barbara asked.

"Just Daddy."

"And did he say he thinks adoption is the best choice?" Richard had said he was being careful not to influence her decision, but could he be doing so without realizing it?

"No. We just talked about babies and how much responsibility they are. He says they turn your life upside down."

"Raising a baby is a very big commitment," Barbara agreed. "Have you ever been around a baby, Missy?"

Missy pulled away, wiping tears from her cheeks with her fingertips. "Heather has a baby brother. He's cute, but sometimes he's a pain. He flushed Heather's best makeup brushes down the toilet and they had to call a plumber because everything got plugged up, and Heather got in trouble because she left them where he could reach them, and her mother said it was a good thing he didn't eat her makeup and get poisoned. Heather and I baby-sat for him once and we had to give him dinner. When he eats, it's disgusting."

"So you know babies aren't always sweet and cuddly."

"Daddy says they're a lot of work, and they always need all kinds of special things—someplace to sleep, and new clothes all the time, and they have to go to the doctor, and if they get sick, they keep you up all night."

"All that's true," Barbara conceded. "And it's good that you realize that when you're trying to decide whether to keep your baby or give it up for adoption. Some girls think that having a baby is like having a living doll, and that the baby will love them no matter what. And then they're disappointed and resentful."

Missy was thoughtful a moment. "If babies are so much trouble, why do people want them?"

Barbara smiled. Another one of those impossible, unanswerable philosophy-of-life questions! "It goes back to what we talked about the other day—about continuing life. It's about giving up part of yourself for someone, and showing what love is, so he or she can grow up and teach the next generation how to love."

"That sounds hard."

"It's not easy. But it's life. And having a baby is a bit of a miracle."

"A miracle?"

"I think you know what I mean. Remember when you felt the baby move for the first time? Or when you saw his face on the monitor? That tingly feeling that made you want to laugh and cry all at the same time?"

Missy nodded.

"Well, that was part of the miracle. It was love you felt. And it's that love that makes people want to raise children."

"Daddy says it's hard to be a parent when you're not ready for it."

"It's hard even when you are." She smiled. "I think I'd like to tell you about a friend of mine. But first, I'm thirsty. Sure you don't want something to drink?"

"Maybe some milk."

"And maybe a peanut butter apple?" Barbara teased.

Missy nodded sheepishly, and they walked together to the kitchen.

"What about your friend?" Missy asked when they were seated.

Barbara grinned. "Her name is Samantha. She was my roommate and best friend in college. She was an accountant and she married an engineer and they became Yuppies, big time. He drove a BMW and she drove a Volvo, and they bought a high-rise condo just outside the city."

She took a bite of apple, chewed and savored it before continuing. "When Samantha turned twenty-nine, she decided that her clock was ticking and that it was time to have a baby. So she went to her doctor and started taking vitamins and read everything she could find on childbearing. She figured out her most fertile time of the month and booked a romantic cruise so she would be relaxed when they made their baby."

"Did she get pregnant?"

"Oh, yes. Somewhere on the high seas between Miami and Nassau. Then she really started reading books, and she bought a special megaphone that pressed against her abdomen so she could talk to her baby. She also bought special tapes to play to soothe the baby inside her. They went to natural childbirth classes and he helped deliver the baby and tie the cord, and they had a beautiful baby girl. Samantha stayed at home six months and then they hired a wonderful nanny and everything was wonderful until Chelsea—that was their daughter—enrolled in pre-kindergarten. At a very progressive private school, of course."

"What happened then?" Missy asked, totally hooked on the story.

"Well, one night Samantha called me. She was hysterical. I could hardly understand her because she was sobbing." Barbara grinned wryly. "It's a wonder her tears didn't short out the speaker phone."

Missy grinned back. "What was wrong?"

"Chelsea's teacher had recommended that they keep Chelsea in pre-kindergarten an extra year because when she drew pictures of people, she didn't put fingers on them."

"What?" Missy asked, her face screwing up with incredulity.

"That's it. Samantha called me because she knew I had a master's in education and she wanted a second opinion. She was sure she'd done something wrong to make Chelsea such a failure, and she wondered if she should ever have become a mother because she was such a miserable failure at it."

"What did you tell her?"

"I told her to relax, because children develop in very individual ways on individual timetables and that eventually Chelsea would notice that people have fingers. I told her to buy Chelsea some paper and crayons and let her draw instead of playing so many intellectually stimulating games with the kid, and to hang

Chelsea's artwork on the refrigerator, whether her people had fingers or not."

"Did she?"

Barbara shrugged. "Yes. And two weeks later she called back and said Chelsea was putting fingers on her stick figures and so the counselors had decided to let her into kindergarten right on schedule. The point is, parenting is a tough job and no matter how old or educated or prepared or capable a parent is, from time to time she's going to feel helpless and inadequate and insecure."

Missy was chewing on her lip again. Barbara concentrated on her apple while Missy mulled over the story. After finishing their milk, they went back to the living room to resume collating and stapling.

"If I give my baby up for adoption, do you think the parents would let him wear the booties we bought for him?"

"I don't know," Barbara said. "I would think so, especially if they knew they were from you. If you wanted to see your baby, you could probably put them on him yourself."

"The pamphlet Dr. Scofield gave me on adoption said that sometimes you can write letters or give gifts to the baby and the new parents can send you pictures of the baby through an attorney."

"Dr. Scofield also said you could meet prospective parents. You could help choose a couple you think would be good to your baby."

Missy stapled and gnawed on her lip. "I would give my baby my *Cat in the Hat* book."

"Is that your favorite?"

Missy nodded. "Daddy used to read it to me every night. He was funny when he read it."

"The way he was when you two were ordering cobbler the other night?"

"Yeah," Missy said, grinning. "He's pretty silly sometimes."

"You're lucky to have a daddy like that."

"Yeah." The change in Missy was abrupt. Almost startling. Her chin quivered. Her shoulders sagged. Her entire body crumpled into a sobbing mass.

Barbara gathered her into her arms and rocked her, stroking her back, murmuring sounds of reassurance. "Let it out, sweetie. Just let it out. You'll feel better afterward."

"I didn't mean to mess up Daddy's life again," Missy wheezed between sobs. "I didn't mean to get pregnant like my mother."

*Like her mother*. Barbara's hair stood on end. What did she really know about Christine? What misconceptions had she been carrying around for God knew how long? How did a vulnerable girl like Missy cope with the knowledge that her mother was the kind of woman Christine had been, flitting from man to man?

"What do you mean, like your mother?" Barbara asked.

Missy pulled away, sniffing and wiping her face with her fingertips. "You won't tell?" she asked. "You said everything I told you is confidential."

"That's right." God, how had she gotten herself into this compromising situation?

Missy sniffed again. "Daddy was going to college to become a lawyer, and he would have, but he dropped out to take care of me instead, and it was all her fault."

"Your mother's?"

Middy nodded frantically. "She seduced him and got pregnant on purpose so he would have to marry her."

"Who told you all this?" Barbara asked.

"Nobody told me. I heard my grandmother talking to my daddy. Lots of times."

Missy lunged for Barbara, throwing her arms around Barbara's neck and sobbing bitterly against her shoulder. "She was always afraid I would turn out like my mother. She said that's why I liked to dress so ... so ... provocatively and wear so much makeup and spike up my hair."

"Oh, Missy," Barbara groaned, rocking her. "Oh, sweetheart. Your grandmother—"

"She was right," Missy sobbed. "I'm pregnant just like my mother was, and my daddy's life is all messed up again."

"But this situation is different, Missy. You weren't promiscuous like—" She caught herself before she used Christine's name, but it was too late.

Once again, Missy pulled back. Her chest was heaving as she drew in a labored breath, struggling for composure. "You did know her, didn't you? You knew my mother was a slut."

Her face crumpled again, and Barbara pulled her back into a hug. "Slut is a strong word, Missy. I didn't know your mother well, but I know she didn't have a family who cared about her. She wasn't bad, not the way you think. She just never had anyone to teach her decency and self-respect. And there's no way she could have been a totally bad person and have such a wonderful daughter."

She pushed a strand of Missy's hair away from her cheek, where it had become plastered against a tear. "Missy, you didn't inherit tainted blood. You aren't responsible for anything your mother did, and you're not a bad person because you made love with your boyfriend."

"If I don't give up my baby, Daddy's life is going to be turned upside down all over again, the way it was when I was born."

"Oh, sweetheart, if your dad's torn up about your being pregnant, it's because he's concerned about what having a baby would do to your life, not to his. You two need to talk this over a lot more before you make any decisions that will influence the rest of your lives."

She held the troubled teenager, rocking her gently in her arms, until she felt the girl relax. Gradually, she drew her arms from around Missy, letting the teenager pull away at her own pace. Then she fetched a box of tissues.

After a while, she and Missy finished collating and stapling the information packets. Shortly after that, Missy left. Before her car was even out of sight, Barbara was dialing Richard's office number.

HE CAME OVER at nine o'clock.

"How's Missy?" Barbara asked.

"She's okay," Richard replied. "I took your advice and took her out to dinner. She was a little quiet, but she has been lately." He gave her a questioning look.

"What's this about, Barbara? After your call, I was expecting her to be hysterical."

"I was the one who was hysterical. We had a rough visit today." Barbara looked at him beseechingly. "I could probably tolerate a hug right about now."

"God, Barbara. Come here. I could use a little one-on-one myself." Barbara melted against him. "You smell good," he said, burrowing his face in her hair.

"Press a button," Barbara pleaded as his hands worked magic kneading her shoulders. "Make the world go away."

"If I knew where the button was, I'd push it so fast we'd have whiplash." He hesitated almost a full minute before bringing the world crashing down on them again by asking, "What's going on with Missy?"

"Let's sit down," Barbara said, leading him to the couch.

"If we have to sit down first, it must be serious."

"It is," Barbara said flatly. "Missy—" Finding the words difficult, she exhaled wearily and started over, with new determination. "Missy is considering giving the baby up for adoption."

"We knew that," Richard said. Confused, he searched Barbara's face. "You can't be surprised? Barbara, we've known all along that adoption was an option. I know you've become involved with this baby, but you've got to realize—"

"It's not that she's considering adoption," Barbara said. "It's *why*."

"Why?" Richard said, more perplexed than ever. "She's probably beginning to realize that she's not ready to be a mother."

Barbara peered into his eyes. "If that were why she was thinking about giving away her baby, I wouldn't be upset—if she thought it would be best for the baby and for her own future."

"What other reason would she have?"

Barbara's expression was tragic. Richard could almost feel her reluctance to answer.

"She's protecting you," she said.

"Me?"

"She thinks—" Barbara said, then buried her face in her hands and groaned. "Oh, Richard. I'm so conflicted."

"Conflicted?"

Barbara let her hands fall into her lap and shook her head slowly before meeting Richard's concerned gaze. "I don't know what or how much I should tell you."

"If it concerns Missy, you can tell me anything."

"I can't violate the confidence of a student, especially one I care so strongly about."

"The student in question happens to be my daughter."

Barbara's eyes narrowed. "I am morally and ethically bound to respect Missy's privacy."

"And I'm her father! I have a right to know anything that affects her well-being. If there's something you're keeping from me—"

Barbara sighed as if she were a balloon deflating. "Let's not argue. We're on the same side. Missy's side. We both want what's best for her. We should be working together, not sniping at each other."

"I'm sorry. You just . . . I've been on edge since you called. It's just so damned frustrating seeing Missy in so much trouble and feeling like there's not a thing I can do to help her. And when you insinuate that there's some deep, dark secret—"

"There's not any deep, dark secret. Missy just told me some things that led me to believe she's carrying around a lot of guilt."

"Guilt? What has she got to feel guilty about? She was just following good old dad's example."

Barbara mulled that over a long time before responding. "I don't think Missy's decision to have sex had anything to do with finding you on the sofa with a stranger. She's a teenager, with teenage hormones, teenage curiosity, and teenage peer pressure all around her—and she thought she was in love." She ventured a smile. "You remember what that was like, don't you?"

Richard was astonished to find himself smiling back. "Only too well."

Barbara reached for his hand and held it between hers. "Remember when your mother found lipstick on your collar after the homecoming dance and said no nice girl would wear lipstick that dark?"

"I'd forgotten all about that."

Barbara traced the length of his fingers, one by one, with her fingertip. "I think my attitude toward your mother is compromising my objectivity."

Richard's mouth hardened into a frown. "Has Missy been talking about my mother?"

"She mentions her from time to time. She loves your mother." She had been drawing imaginary circles on the top of his hand. She stopped abruptly, and said thoughtfully, "Sometimes the people we care about the most have the greatest power to influence our thinking. Or shape perceptions."

"What kind of perceptions are we talking about?"

"Oh, about people and situations."

"Any specific people or situations?"

Barbara hesitated before answering. "Do you want Missy to give up her baby?"

"What?" Richard said, perplexed both by the question and the abrupt change of direction in the conversation.

"Is it what you want for her?"

"I want what's best for her."

"That's a cop-out answer. It's just you and me here. Tell me what you really want her to do, deep down inside."

Sadness haunted Richard's eyes. "I want to wake up tomorrow morning and discover this whole thing has been a nightmare and she's not pregnant at all."

"That's not on the list of choices."

"Yeah. Well, the real choices on the list suck swamp water. I think about her trying to raise a child single-handedly and I'm terrified for her. And then I think about her giving her baby away and I'm just as terrified, because I know she'd never be the same person again."

"Which prospect terrifies you the most?"

His eyes searched hers. For compassion. For understanding. "Are you a counselor now, or a woman?"

"I'm the woman who loves you."

He reached for her and wrapped his arms around her tightly as if she were a lifeline. "Tell me what to do. I've made too many mistakes already. God, Barbara, don't let me screw this up, too."

She kissed him—his neck, his cheeks, his eyelids—and as she kissed him, she caressed him with her hands, smoothing his hair and shoulders. "You're going to do what's best for Missy. You're going to be there for her, supporting her. *We're* going to be there for her."

Slowly they released each other, but they remained close, with Barbara sitting across his lap and their faces just inches apart. Barbara swallowed, struggling for composure as she gathered her thoughts. "Missy... when you and Missy talked about how a baby might change her life, did you mention that you'd wanted to be a lawyer and had to give it up when Christine became pregnant?"

"What? No! Of course not. We talked about Missy's wanting to go to FSU, not about—"

Barbara's shoulders drooped as she sighed wearily. "That's what I thought."

Richard looked questioningly into her eyes. "Is that what you meant when you said Missy feels guilty?"

Barbara nodded gravely. "She has this idea that you were an innocent drawn into a web of seduction, and if not for her—"

"I've never told her that. I'd never tell her anything like that. She doesn't even know Christine was pregnant before she and I got married."

"Your mother never talked about Christine? Not even when Missy was little, or when she might have been in the next room? There was never tension between you and Christine when she came to visit Missy?"

Richard shook his head helplessly. Sadly.

"Children don't have to be told some things, Richard. They absorb information through some sort of osmosis. They tune in to attitudes and pick up snatches and snippets of conversation, and sometimes partial truths get all tangled up with perceptions, and a fertile imagination fills in the blanks."

Richard groaned. "I thought things couldn't get any worse." His gaze met hers evenly, searching for answers. "How do we help her?"

Her eyes grew limpid with tears. "It's not going to be easy."

Richard chortled bitterly. "Like I even remember what that word means."

"I think you should talk to Missy about you and Christine. I think she needs to know the whole story."

Richard's heart was in his throat. "It's ancient history, Barbara. What possible good would it do for Missy to know—?"

"That when her father was young and inexperienced, he succumbed to peer pressure and made an error in judgment? I can't think of anything Missy needs to know more." She framed his face in her hands, pleading with her eyes. "She adores you, Richard. She feels like she's let you down. If you let her know that you're fallible enough to make a mistake, then maybe she can believe that you can understand how she could make one and love her in spite of it."

"Missy knows I love her."

"Of course she does. Because you're her perfect father, and perfect fathers love their daughters. She knows you'll love her even if she messes up your life the way her mother did. But think how much more it would mean to her to know that you're imperfect enough to understand what she's going through. Think what it'll mean to her if she knows that you're with her, no matter what, even if she makes her decisions based on what's good for her and the baby instead of what's good for you."

"Is she really doing that?"

Her face strained with the effort of holding back tears, Barbara nodded, then fell forward, looping her arms around his neck and burying her cheek against his shoulder. "Yes. And someday, after she's spent Christmas after Christmas and birthday after birthday wondering about the child she gave up, she's going to realize it, and when that happens, she's going to resent you, because she's going to realize that she didn't have a choice, not a real one. But if you do this for her . . ."

She leaned back so she could see his face. "If you give her a real choice, she's going to love you even more than she already loves you."

He folded his arms around her once again, drawing on her strength as he held her tightly against him. "You make it sound as if I'm standing at the bedside ready to wrest the child out of her arms like some Victorian curmudgeon."

"You're as far removed from a Victorian curmudgeon as you could possibly be," Barbara assured him. "And Missy knows that. Ironically, your loving support feeds into the misconception she's developed over her lifetime."

His sigh rattled her ear. "Life is so very . . . complicated."

"Would it help if I told you I love you?"

"Help? You're my rock. I don't know how I would have made it through this without you."

"But will you still love me when you don't need me so desperately?" Barbara was only half teasing.

"I've loved you since the first time I saw you, and nothing—not time or separation or stupid mistakes or anything else—is ever going to change that. Finding you again, when I needed you most, has been . . . it's been like stepping out of dense fog into sunlight. But if I hadn't found you last month—if it had been next month, or next year—I would have fallen in love with you all over again, the way I do every time I see your face."

Barbara's throat was too tight, her heart too full for speech, so she clung to him, letting him know by her closeness what was in her heart. Several minutes passed in a silence rich with their wordless communion.

"What are we going to do if she keeps the baby?" Richard asked at length.

"Love it, of course," Barbara replied. "And keep on loving Missy, so she knows she's not alone."

"It's so daunting," Richard said. "The idea of a baby in the house. The noise and confusion and the sleepless nights and the constant demands—"

"You managed with Missy."

"I was younger then. I had more energy. I didn't realize how difficult parenting was. I just did it."

"And you'll help Missy do it the same way. And I'll help you and it'll be crazy, but we'll do it because we're a family, and that's what families are for."

"I like the sound of that," he said.

"There's only one real problem that I can see."

"I'm almost afraid to ask," he said. "If there's something I haven't thought of already, I'm not sure I want to know."

Barbara giggled. "It's that you look too young to be a grandfather. No one's going to believe you! Grandfathers are supposed to have gray hair and carve squirrels out of blocks of wood."

He cradled her head in his hands and looked lovingly down at her face. "You may be the only person in the world who could make me smile right now. But I gotta tell you—you aren't going to have any more credibility than I do. You're going to be the sexiest grandma in history."

"You can buy me a flannel nightie."

Richard laughed in earnest. "This is Florida. No one wears flannel nighties here. How about something . . . *lacy* that I can see through?"

"Is that any way for a grandfather to talk?"

"It is when he's got a woman like you in his lap."

The pleasantness of the interlude lingered through several minutes of silence before Barbara sensed the tension creeping back into Richard's body. "What time is it?" he asked.

"Ten-thirty. Will Missy be awake when you get home?"

"I don't know. She used to be a night owl, but now she sometimes tucks in around ten." He paused, then asked, "I really have to do it, don't I?"

Barbara nodded against his chest, and Richard sighed. "Where am I going to find the strength?"

"You have the strength inside you. It's mixed in with the love you have for Missy. You'll find it." She threaded her fingers through his and kissed his mouth gently. "And after you do, you'll be closer to Missy than ever."

She walked with Richard to the door a few minutes later. "I'll only be a phone call away," she said. "Let me know how it goes."

Richard nodded and gave her a quick good-night kiss before leaving.

Barbara went through her nightly bedtime routine, but as she settled into bed to read, she found it impossible to concentrate on a complicated journal article while her mind was preoccupied with Richard and Missy. Richard was probably home by now; he and Missy could be talking at this very minute.

The ring of the phone startled her out of deep thought, and a sense of ill ease lingered with her as she lifted the receiver and said hello.

"Missy's sound asleep," Richard said without preamble. "I don't want to wake her up tonight. I'll talk to her tomorrow."

"That may be better," Barbara said. "You'll have some time to think about how you want to approach it."

"I'm coming back to your place, Barbara. I called so you could watch for me. I don't want to ring the doorbell and get your neighbor's dog all riled up."

"Tonight? This late?"

"It's all right. My neighbor, Cynthia Munoz—the woman you saw at the basketball game—is coming over to sleep on the sofa in case Missy wakes up or there's an emergency. She doesn't mind. She owes me a few favors."

"Oh," Barbara said, vividly recalling the image of Richard lifting Eddie Munoz's father from the wheelchair.

"I can leave your place in time to get home before Missy wakes up in the morning," he said. "Please, Barbara. If you don't want me to come, I won't. But I just . . . I need your arms around me. I want to be with you. All night."

She waited for him in her nightshirt, without bothering with a robe. Silently she reached for his hand when he arrived, and they went to the bedroom together. She got back into bed while he undressed.

"I don't feel like a stud tonight," he warned, settling into bed beside her. "I just want you next to me."

Barbara snuggled up to him, nestling her cheek on his shoulder. "I'm not going anywhere."

Why would she, when there was nowhere else on earth she'd rather be than next to Richard?

# 13

BARBARA KISSED Richard's cheek. "Richard." His other cheek. "Richard." His lips. "Richard."

His eyes flew open. He tensed in an instant of disorientation, then relaxed as he remembered where he was.

"The alarm just rang," Barbara said apologetically.

A slow smile spread over Richard's face. "I like your method better than an alarm clock."

"I hated to wake you. You were sleeping so peacefully." He hadn't even stirred when the alarm went off, or when she'd gotten out of bed to go to the bathroom.

"It was the company," he said a bit groggily.

"It was nice, waking up and finding you here," she said, "then remembering what it was like to fall asleep touching you."

He pulled her into a fierce embrace and rolled atop her. "This is the way it's supposed to be between us. The way it was meant to be. The way it's going to be."

His intensity spoke as eloquently as his words. As did his sensuous growl as he clamped his arms around her even more tightly. "We should have set the alarm thirty minutes earlier."

Barbara grinned tauntingly. "What for?"

"We'll just have to make the most of the few minutes we have," he said with single-minded determination.

"I don't think that's going to be a problem," Barbara said.

It wasn't.

Later, propped up on the pillows, she watched Richard dress. He paused between shirt buttons. "Is something wrong?"

"No," she said with a bittersweet smile. "Something's right. It's . . . the ordinary things."

He sat down on the edge of the bed and took her hand in his. "I meant what I said earlier. This is the way it was meant to be."

Barbara smiled and a mellow silence, filled with the promise of their future, followed. But they could not ignore the present for long.

Richard's expression was solemn as he wove his fingers between hers.

"I may keep Missy out of school today. I don't want to put off talking to her until this afternoon, and I don't think the hour we have before school would be enough."

"That's probably a good idea. You don't want to rush the kind of talk you two need to have. Missy can afford to miss one day of school."

Richard sighed tiredly. "Do you know how much I wish I could crawl back under those covers and spend the day in bed with you?"

"Sooner or later you'd have to get out of bed and deal with reality. You have to face this."

His jaw muscle twitched as he nodded grimly, and as he got up from the bed, he moved with a wooden dread.

"I'll be thinking about you," Barbara said. "Call me when you get a chance. I'll make sure they know to put through the call immediately."

A cursory nod was his only reply.

BARBARA WAS DISTRACTED all day, waiting to hear from Richard and growing increasingly apprehensive with each passing hour. The afternoon progressed and still there was no news. After school she drove home to continue waiting. And fretting.

The phone rang just after five o'clock.

"Is Missy all right?" she asked frantically as soon as she recognized Richard's voice.

"She's fine."

"When I didn't hear anything, I was afraid something might have happened. I almost called Dr. Scofield's office to make sure Missy hadn't been rushed to the hospital."

"Don't you think I would have called if there had been an emergency?"

Barbara's languid sigh slid through the lines. "I'm sorry. When I didn't hear anything, I panicked."

"Missy and I just got home. We spent the day at the beach."

"The beach?"

"It seemed like the best place to have a heart-to-heart talk."

"You sound—" She couldn't decide on a word. Relieved? Ebullient? "How did it go?"

"Very well. But I don't want to go into it over the phone, and Missy wants to be in on our discussion. Can you come over here?"

"To your house?"

"We would both enjoy the pleasure of your company," he said with playful formality.

She was still mulling over Richard's abrupt change of attitude and mood as she rang the Benson doorbell. When he'd left her at 6:00 a.m. he'd been like a man taking the walk from death row to the gas chamber. And now he sounded...relieved wasn't a strong enough word.

They both came to the door. Richard was smiling. Missy greeted her with a hug before leading her into the family room, the back wall of which was a series of glass panels that overlooked the infamous atrium. Barbara tried not to think about Richard's interrupted tryst as she sat down next to Missy on the sofa.

Anticipation grew thick in the room, but no one spoke. Barbara spied the pictures of Missy's baby in the ceramic frames on the coffee table and remembered holding Missy's hand during the sonogram, then going with Richard to buy the frames.

The silence stretched on. It seemed to Barbara almost as though they were all afraid to breach the volatile silence and yet, at the same time, she sensed that Richard and Missy were as close to bursting with the need to tell her what was going on as she was with curiosity to find out.

Finally, unable to stand the pressure any longer, Barbara turned to Missy with an encouraging smile. "I hear you played hooky today and went to the beach."

Missy grinned sheepishly. "You won't tell, will you? I didn't have any tests today, and I'll make up all my work."

"Missy and I wanted to get away for a while," Richard said. "We've always done our best talking and thinking at the beach."

"Your secret's safe with me," Barbara told Missy in a conspiratorial tone. It was good to have dissipated some of the tension, especially when another prolonged silence ensued.

"Missy and I had a long talk," Richard said finally. "She understands a lot of things better now."

Missy concurred with a gentle nod.

"Missy's reached a very important decision. Missy, do you want to tell her?"

As Missy nodded, her eyes were those of a frightened child, and Barbara was reminded of how young the girl truly was, despite the fact that she was pregnant.

"I'm not ready to be a mother," Missy said. "I want to be able to go out with my friends, and after high school I want to go to FSU and live in the dorms. Someday, when I'm older and meet the right person, I can get married and have children when I'm ready for them."

Barbara's gaze locked meaningfully with Richard's before she turned her attention back to Missy. "That sounds like a very mature decision, sweetheart."

"I want to let someone very special adopt my baby."

Barbara's heart ached for Missy and the tiny being inside her, but she forced herself not to let Missy see what she was feeling, especially when Missy's chin quivered. Missy didn't need sympathy, she needed strength and support.

Missy looked at Richard, who nodded encouragement; then she turned back to Barbara. "I want . . . *you* to adopt my baby." A tear trickled down her cheek. "You and Daddy."

Blinking back her own tears, Barbara looked questioningly at Richard.

He grinned self-consciously and shrugged. "The cat's out of the bag, Barbaloo. She knows all about us."

"Oh," Barbara said. "Oh-h-h-h." It was not eloquent, but it was sincere. And it was the only sound she was capable of as she threw her arms around Missy and, rocking her, succumbed to her own tears.

"There's no one else I'd rather give it to," Missy said. "You'll be a good mother. Oh, Ms. Wilson, I'm so glad it could be you."

Countless minutes passed before their tears were spent and sobs gave way to an occasional sniff. "Do you mind if I talk to your father alone for a moment?" Barbara asked, pulling away slightly.

Grinning, Missy shook her head. "I don't mind. You guys probably have a lot you need to discuss. I'll be in my room if you need me."

She sounded so adult and . . . *parental* that Barbara couldn't hold back a smile of pure affection for the teenager as she watched her walk from the room.

Then, suddenly it seemed, Barbara and Richard were alone. For a moment they sat staring at each other like figures in a painting. Then Barbara swallowed. "You told her about us?"

"We'd already talked about everything else. About Christine and . . ." He paused to collect his thoughts. "We were talking about adoption. Open adoption, where she could meet the adoptive mother, and she said, 'You know what, Daddy? I wish Ms. Wilson was married.'"

"She said that?"

Richard nodded. "It floored me, too. When I had recovered from the surprise, I asked her why, and she said, 'Because then she could adopt my baby.'"

He smiled so sweetly that Barbara felt a brush of fresh moisture on her cheeks as she smiled back at him. Although they were close enough to touch hands if they'd reached for each other, he seemed much too far away.

"She said," he continued, "that you understood what a mother was supposed to be, and that you wanted children for the right reasons, and that if you were married, you could adopt her baby."

Barbara was too overcome by emotion to speak.

Richard continued. "Well, it had been a day for truth and revelation, so it seemed natural to say, 'I didn't just know Barbara in high school. We were in love. And when we met each other again, we realized that we still care about each other, and I've asked her to marry me.'"

Barbara swallowed. "Wh-what did she say?"

"She was surprised."

"I'll bet."

He laughed. "She wanted to know if you'd said yes. And then there was a lot of hugging and some mention of the fact that you'd be her stepmother, and then the subject of adoption came up again. She asked if I thought you'd want to adopt the baby, and if I would agree to it if you did."

Barbara drew in a ragged breath. Her chest felt tight. "And what did you say?"

"I told her I was pretty sure you'd be delighted by the idea." He waited for some reaction, then asked, "Aren't you?"

Barbara forced herself to reply calmly. "You know how I feel about Missy's baby."

Richard chuckled nervously. "Does that mean we're going to be parents?"

"That depends on you." She was afraid—afraid to believe it might really be happening. Afraid to believe that Richard could want it as much as she.

"Me?"

"Yesterday you found the prospect of a baby in the house pretty daunting."

"It's my grandchild, Barbara. My flesh and blood. Do you think I could turn him away?"

"Not turning a child away is not exactly the same as wanting one. Parenthood is teamwork, Richard, like marriage. I won't settle for anything less than a full, participating partner."

She followed his gaze to the pictures in the baby blue ceramic frames, and caught the brightness of tears in his eyes before he blinked them away. "I've gotten used to the little guy's face," he said. "I don't want to miss out on watching him grow up."

"It would have to be an adoption in the truest sense. We'd be his parents and Missy would be his sister. Missy would have to understand that."

"She understands. We talked about that for some time. She thinks it's the very best solution. And so do I."

His gaze met hers steadfastly. "It just feels right, Barbara. I missed a lot of the joy and wonder of parenthood the first time around. This time I'm more ready for it, emotionally, financially, every which way."

"You're sure?" she asked, still absorbing the full implications of the situation, allowing herself to hope.

"This time, I'd be sharing the experience with someone I love. Besides—" He grinned. "Missy's going to be going off to school. The baby you and I have together will need a playmate around."

"The baby you and I have?"

His gaze was penetrating. "Do you think I could marry you, knowing how much you want to have a child, and deny you that experience?"

Barbara was trembling. "I didn't think . . . I couldn't bring it up when you were so involved with Missy's problem, but I didn't really think you would want to start all over again with a baby."

"And you were going to marry me anyway?"

"I spent too many years without you not to appreciate being with you," she said, then paused briefly to draw in a fortifying breath. "Before you came back into my life, I'd already come to terms with the fact that I'd never bear a child."

Her eyes met his with unwavering intensity. "I'd rather spend the rest of my life with you, being your wife and Missy's stepmother, than living without you or a child."

"And now you're going to have it all."

Barbara was too filled with joy to sit still another moment. Rising, she held out her arms. "Do you think the woman who's going to have it all could start with a hug? Because—" she succumbed to a sob of pure emotion "—I could sure use one."

Richard rose, spread his arms and said with a flourish, "Come to papa, sweetheart!"

"Oh, Richard!" she said, burying her face against his chest, packing into those two words, a joyous expletive and the breathless pronouncement of his name, love and hope and expectation enough to last a lifetime.

"Better?" Richard asked after holding her for a long moment.

"Mmm," Barbara said. "It just needs one thing to make it perfect."

"What's that?"

"Missy."

"Is that all?" he asked, then shouted with full paternal authority, "Missy! Get your tail in here. Right now!"

The teenager was there in an instant, wide-eyed and apprehensive. His voice softened as he smiled at her. "Your new mother wants a three-way hug."

Missy ran to them and threw an arm across each of their shoulders. They teetered and swayed as a single entity, clinging to one another, supporting one another.

"This is a family thing, isn't it?" Missy asked.

"Yes," Barbara and Richard said in unison, and then laughed.

"I like it," Missy said. "A lot."

"So do I, sweetie," Barbara said, her eyes meeting Richard's above Missy's head. "So do I."

# Epilogue

BARBARA GASPED as the transmission gel plopped onto her abdomen.

"Aw, come on—it's not even cold!" the technician teased. "Relax!"

"I'm a little excited," Barbara said.

"You have a right to be," the technician said, sliding the transducer into the gel. "It's not every day you get a first glimpse of your baby's face."

A flurry of motion drew their attention to the door.

"What's this?" he said. "We've got the entire family. I'm going to start selling tickets!"

Missy came into the room, followed by Richard, who was cradling a toddler in his arms.

"It's about time you showed up!" Barbara said with mock severity.

Richard leaned over and kissed her on the forehead. "We had a diaper emergency, so I was in the bathroom when the nurse came to get us."

"Were you a stinky boy?" Barbara asked the toddler.

"Puu-uuey!" the toddler said, holding his nose.

Barbara chuckled. "You little ham!"

"Puu-uuey!" the toddler repeated.

Barbara groaned and rolled her eyes. "What are we going to do with two at the same time?"

"Love them," Richard said, smiling broadly. "And stock up on vitamins."

"I'm looking for a face," the technician said. "There's an arm in the way. If the little fellow will just move a li-tt-le bit."

Barbara, Richard and Missy stared at the monitor with rapt attention. Barbara grasped Missy's hand.

"There!" the technician said exuberantly. "Eyes, nose and mouth!"

"Oh!" Barbara said. "Oh, Richard, Missy, look! Willy, do you see the face. That's your baby brother. Or sister."

"Which is it?" Missy asked.

"Let's find out," the technician said, slowly moving the transducer, pointing out arms and legs. Finally he paused the transducer. "Looks like a brother to me!"

"A boy!" Richard said with a delighted chuckle. "What do you think of that, Willy? You're going to have a baby brother."

"Baby in Mommy's tummy," Willy said, his eyes, so like Missy's, twinkling as he spoke.

"That's right," Richard said. "Mommy has your baby brother in her tummy."

"Love the baby," Willy said.

"Yes, we do," Barbara said. "We love the baby just like we love Missy and Willy."

"You may feel some pressure while I do these measurements," the technician said, but he went largely ignored.

"It's going to be pure pandemonium with two boys in the house," Richard said. "Missy, don't you want to go to college locally so you can stay at home and help out?"

"No way!" Missy said. "If this baby is as rowdy as Willy, I'd never get any studying done!"

Richard and Barbara exchanged amused grins, but Missy turned serious. "I'm glad you had your sonogram before I left for Tallahassee."

"I insisted," Barbara said. "After all, this baby is your brother."

"Do you think I could have a picture of him to go with the family portrait we had done?" Missy asked. Meeting Barbara's eyes, she squeezed Barbara's hand and smiled. "I want to be able to see both my brothers every day."

"Of course you may have a picture," Barbara said.

The next morning Richard, Barbara and Willy stood in the front yard waving goodbye to Missy. As her car, loaded to capacity with the clothing, stereo equipment and other items essential to a college freshman, disappeared from view, Richard said, "I know she has to grow up. And I know she's doing what's good for her. But I'm going to miss her."

Barbara stretched her arm across his waist. "Even with Willy here, the house is going to seem empty without her," she agreed.

"Not nearly as empty..." Richard said, letting his voice trail off. After a beat of thoughtful silence, he began again. "When I think of how empty it would have been if I hadn't found you again, it makes my gut tie up in knots."

"But you did find me," Barbara said. "And we have Willy, and the new baby—"

He spread his hand over her rounded abdomen and smiled. "Yes," he said. "But they're only ours until they grow up and go off to live their own lives. You and I—"

"Are never going to have to waste our energy on regrets or wondering what might have been," she finished for him.

"It's strange," he said. "We lost all those years, and yet now, we have it all. Everything except the years we can't bring back. Do you think . . . ?"

"What?" she asked.

"That in some crazy way, we appreciate it more because of those lost years?"

"I know I do," she said.

"I guess I do, too."

"That just leaves one problem," Barbara said.

"What?" Richard asked, showing his alarm.

"We have to decide which of us is going to get that water hose away from Willy." She bobbed her head toward the corner of the yard, where Willy was attempting to turn the handle of the water faucet with scrunch-faced determination.

"Not again!" Richard said. "Willy!" He jogged toward the toddler, but he was too late. The faucet yielded and Willy picked up the garden hose and waved it wildly through the air. By the time Richard was able to wrest the hose away from him and turn off the water, father and son were drenched.

"Daddy all wet!" Willy said, giggling delightedly from the security of his father's arms.

"He sure is," Barbara said, laughing at the aggrieved scowl on Richard's face. "But we love him, anyway, don't we?"

"Love Daddy," Willy repeated, and Barbara could only nod in agreement as she watched Richard's expression soften with a father's tolerant love.

Poor Richard. He was such a marshmallow. But then—that was one of the reasons she loved him so much.

# HARLEQUIN®
## *Temptation*®
## IS TEN!

Join the festivities as Harlequin celebrates
Temptation's tenth anniversary in 1994!

Look for tempting treats from your favorite
Temptation authors all year long. The celebration
begins with Passion's Quest—four exciting sensual
stories featuring the most elemental passions....

The temptation continues with Lost Loves, a sizzling
miniseries about love lost...love found. And watch for
the 500th Temptation in July by bestselling author
Rita Clay Estrada, a seductive story in the vein
of the much-loved tale, THE IVORY KEY.

In May, look for details of an irresistible offer:
three classic Temptation novels by Rita Clay Estrada,
Glenda Sanders and Gina Wilkins in a collector's
hardcover edition—free with proof of purchase!

After ten tempting years, *nobody* can resist

## *Temptation*®

**Where do you find hot Texas nights, smooth Texas charm and dangerously sexy cowboys?**

Crystal Creek reverberates with the exciting rhythm of Texas. Each story features the rugged individuals who live and love in the Lone Star state.

"...Crystal Creek wonderfully evokes the hot days and steamy nights of a small Texas community...impossible to put down until the last page is turned."
—*Romantic Times*

"...a series that should hook any romance reader. Outstanding."
—*Rendezvous*

"Altogether, it couldn't be better."  —*Rendezvous*

Don't miss the next book in this exciting series.
**SHAMELESS by SANDY STEEN**

Available in July wherever Harlequin books are sold.

HARLEQUIN®

*Temptation*

*Lost Loves*

## RIGHT MAN...WRONG TIME

Remember that one man who turned your world upside down. Who made you experience all the ecstatic highs of passion and lows of loss and regret. What if you met him again?

You dared to lose your heart once and had it broken. Dare you love again?

JoAnn Ross, Glenda Sanders, Rita Clay Estrada, Gina Wilkins and Carin Rafferty. Find their stories in Lost Loves, Temptation's newest miniseries, running May to September 1994.

In July, experience *Forms of Love* by Rita Clay Estrada, Book #500 from Temptation! Dan Lovejoy had lost his wife in a tragic accident—then he met her double. Only this woman who looked like Kendra wasn't Kendra. Moreover, she had some very *unusual* secrets of her own. Dan couldn't help himself—he started to fall in love with her. But who was he falling in love with? A moving, romantic story in the tradition of *The Ivory Key*.

## What if...?

LOST3

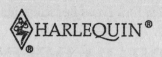

## EXPECTATIONS
### Shannon Waverly

Eternity, Massachusetts, is a town with something special going for it. According to legend, those who marry in Eternity's chapel are destined for a lifetime of happiness. As long as the legend holds true, couples will continue to flock here to marry and local businesses will thrive.

Unfortunately for the town, Marion and Geoffrey Kent are about to prove the legend wrong!

**EXPECTATIONS,** available in July from Harlequin Romance®, is the second book in Harlequin's new cross-line series, **WEDDINGS, INC.** Be sure to look for the third book, **WEDDING SONG,** by Vicki Lewis Thompson (Harlequin Temptation® #502), coming in August.

*New York Times* Bestselling Author

# BARBARA DELINSKY

**Look for her at your favorite retail outlet this
September with**

## A SINGLE ROSE

A two-week Caribbean treasure hunt with rugged and
sexy Noah VanBaar wasn't Shaye Burke's usual style.
Stuck with Noah on a beat-up old sloop with no engine,
she was left feeling both challenged and confused. Torn
between passion and self-control, Shaye was afraid of
being swept away by an all-consuming love.

**Available in September, wherever Harlequin books are sold.**

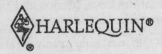

HARLEQUIN®

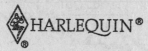